Flying with a Broken Wing

LAURA BEST

NIMBUS
PUBLISHING

For Mum

Nimbus Publishing Limited
3731 Mackintosh St, Halifax, NS B3K 5A5
(902) 455-4286 nimbus.ca

*This novel is a work of fiction. Names, characters, places, and incidents are either the
product of the author's imagination or are used fictitiously.*
NB 1098

Printed and bound in Canada
Design: Heather Bryan
Author photo: Shelley Zinck

MIX
Paper from
responsible sources
FSC® C013916

Library and Archives Canada Cataloguing in Publication

Best, Laura, author
Flying with a broken wing / Laura Best.

Issued in print and electronic formats.
ISBN 978-1-77108-038-5 (pbk.).—ISBN 978-1-77108-039-2 (pdf).—
ISBN 978-1-77108-041-5 (mobi).—ISBN 978-1-77108-040-8 (epub)

I. Title.

PS8603.E777F59 2013   jC813'.6   C2013-903454-4
                                    C2013-903455-2

The Canada Council Le Conseil des Arts
for the Arts du Canada

NOVA SCOTIA
Communities, Culture and Heritage

Nimbus Publishing acknowledges the financial support for its publishing activities from
the Government of Canada through the Canada Book Fund (CBF) and the Canada
Council for the Arts, and from the Province of Nova Scotia through the Department of
Communities, Culture and Heritage.

"A bird can't fly with a broken wing, Cammie Deveau, no more than you can do the things the rest of us can," Aunt Millie said, the day I asked why I couldn't go to school like everyone else, and for the longest while I believed her.

Prologue

From as far back as I can remember I'd lie in bed at night and wonder what my next life would be like. I'd dream up a brand new colour for my hair and a fancy new way to style it. I'd dream up being tall or short, thin or fat, depending upon how I was feeling at the time. I'd be the one in charge, the one who got to do the choosing. I'd stroll along, point my finger, and say, "I'll take one of those, please and thank you." Like a big old store where they'd dole you out anything you could possibly want—that's how I'd get to choose my life.

One thing I'd always make sure to dream up for myself was a set of good strong eyes. I wasn't about to start out with that against me again. I wouldn't even be picky on the colour so long as they matched. If you're too fussy for your own good, chances are you'll end up with nothing. I knew as long as I could see the Milky Way and the face of the man on the moon I'd be happy.

Once I had all the physical details straightened away in my head—like height, weight, hair colour, and so on—I'd go to work on the rest of my life. I'd dream up a nice fine place to live; some fancy house with indoor plumbing and the works, window boxes for growing flowers in, maybe even wooden shutters. Then to prove I wasn't being selfish and wanting all the best for myself, some nights I'd dream up your run-of-the-mill house, my very own mother and father standing in the doorway waiting for me to come home, each of them wearing a big old smile on their face just for me. It wouldn't take a whole lot to make me happy. I'd be willing to compromise on most of the details, so long as there was someone at home who really cared.

The best place I liked to dream up for myself was a spot down by the sea with waves slapping the shore, where bits of driftwood collected on the sand. I'd dream up a bunch of gulls for in the sky and have them making a godawful racket while they swooped above the water. And then there'd be me on some fancy boat out on the Atlantic. Oh, I could get used to that right smartly. Most nights that's how I'd fall to sleep, eyes squeezed together so tight a whisker of light couldn't pry them open.

Then, right before drifting off to sleep, I'd wonder how long I'd have to stay in this life before I got the one I really wanted. As I got older I started to figure out that I couldn't go on waiting for my new life to begin. I couldn't sit back and do nothing. If I didn't want to be stuck living the kind of life I had in Tanner with Aunt Millie, I had to come up with some idea, some way to get out.

Chapter One

"Sit here and don't move," said Aunt Millie, shoving some liquorice candy at me. The bench out near the front door of Mae Cushion's store was none too comfortable. A person would have to have calluses on her rump the size of barn shovels not to complain. Not that I wasn't used to it, given how many hours I'd sat there over the years.

I unrolled one of the liquorice whips and started to gnaw my way to the end. Aunt Millie was scarcely out the door when Mae Cushion started chewing about her.

"I wonder where *she's* taking off to," she said, turning around to gawk out the window. I got off the bench and headed toward the back of the store. Something told me I wouldn't want to sit there and listen to Mae breathing her complaints about Aunt Millie to the woman across the counter.

"Wherever it is, she seems to be in a hurry," said the woman.

"It's a shame for the girl, though."

I snapped my head around. There was a clear view of the counter from where I stood. They weren't even turned my way, yet their whispers circled around me like blowflies on a rotting carcass.

"Poor dear won't know a thing," continued Mae. "Hasn't been to school a day so far."

"Is that allowed?" the woman asked.

"It is if no one says anything. Jeff Chisholm never sent his boy."

"Yes, but he helps out on the farm."

I sashayed over to the next aisle, taking no care to be quiet. My shoes yelled out "I hear you!" as I stomped across the floorboards. Who did they think they were, talking about me that way?

"Mark my words: if she doesn't get some kind of education, she'll end up looking after Millie Turple in her old age. What else can she do, hardly able to see a hand in front of her? Not that Millie Turple would give a flying fig," said Mae.

I moved in a bit closer, curious about what else they had to say. Why do people think if you can't see well your hearing must be bad too?

When the woman at the counter made a *t-t-t*ing sound, a queer feeling started in my head and worked its way through the rest of me, filling out my arms and legs like water running over rocks. Mae leaned her ugly mug across the counter toward me. The store wasn't that big. I should have ducked out of sight.

"I bet you'd like to go to school, wouldn't you, dear?" she asked in a loud, I-feel-sorry-for-you kind of voice. I stole a glance while pretending to inspect the items on the shelf in front of me. I picked up a can and held it close. Peaches, by the picture on the label.

I could handle an awkward silence better than I could handle a bunch of nosy questions from someone who didn't have the good sense not to whisper about me when I was right there. And anyway, when you're different by a mile, you don't need to follow anyone's rules. I held my tongue. Mae gave a grunt. Believe me, she didn't want to hear what was running through my brain.

"Where *is* her mother?" the woman asked once my silence made it through their thick heads and they realized I wasn't going to answer Mae's question.

"Timbuktu, as far as anyone here knows. I don't think Millie's even sure."

"Why would anyone leave a child for Millie Turple to raise?"

There came more *t-t-t*ing sounds.

"What do you suppose really goes on in that house?" the woman added.

A pinprick caught me below the ribs. I wondered how many people in Sheppard Square knew that Aunt Millie sold moonshine. I wanted to tell them both to just never mind about me. Words ricochet off you or else they sink in deep. If you're good enough at acting, no one knows the difference. Who says there's nothing to be learned from living with a bootlegger all your life?

A quick image smacked me upside the head while I stood examining the cans on the shelf.

Me, emptying Aunt Millie's chamber pail in her old age, spooning porridge over her barenaked gums. Aunt Millie drooling like a big old baby, old and grey and wrinkled to the bone. Me, scrubbing and cleaning and doing all the chores, someone knocking at the back door yelling for me to get them some moonshine.

I wasn't going to let that happen. Before you knew it I'd be grown and Aunt Millie would be old. With no other way to make money, it would fall to me to do all the bootlegging. As much as I hated to admit it, when Mae Cushion told that woman I needed to go to school, she was right. Mae Cushion might have been a meddlesome busybody, but she knew more than Aunt Millie ever would.

—

"Why don't I get to go to school like everyone else?" I asked Aunt Millie a few days later. I was sitting across the kitchen table from Ed Hanover, scribbling on a piece of brown wrapping paper. I already knew how to make my letters, thanks to Herb Winters. He'd printed the alphabet on a shingle a few years back with a piece of lumberman's chalk. I'd practised copying the letters onto paper until I got good at it. But knowing how to make letters didn't help me learn how to read and write words. I knew a few of my sums and take aways from playing with the buttons in Aunt Millie's button box and, when she was in a good mood, Aunt Millie would even play along.

"You've got to be able to count if you want to make change someday," she'd say, smug like she thought I wouldn't know what *that* meant.

"Why the devil are you asking about school?" Aunt Millie demanded.

"Everyone else goes."

I'd been trying to figure out some of the words in those old *Standard* magazines Aunt Millie gave me a while back. Seeing all those photos of the king and queen, not knowing what the words said, put me in hard shape. A picture might be worth a thousand words, but what words? I could stare at them till I got bug-eyed and they still wouldn't make any sense. The only thing I could print was my name.

"And I suppose if everyone else jumped in the lake you'd want to too?"

I didn't lift my head up when Aunt Millie spoke. I had my face up close to the table so that I could see the lovely loops and swirls I was making on the paper. I didn't know a thing about writing, but I figured I should at least show I was interested in learning.

Aunt Millie was at the stove pouring hot water into the teapot. She wouldn't even turn around to face me.

"How's it going?" she'd asked with a spark in her voice when Ed walked in a half hour earlier. I figured he was her new boyfriend, maybe someone from over in Sheppard Square. It was the first time I'd seen him around. He tipped his hat to Aunt Millie, walked right over like he owned the joint, and shook my hand.

"I'm Ed Hanover," he said. "But just call me Ed."

"Should I boil the kettle?" asked Aunt Millie right away.

Boil the kettle? Aunt Millie was offering him a cup of tea? Moonshine, yes, but tea? I figured there must be something different about Ed if she was being all polite and friendly. Maybe he was one of those "keepers" she talked about finding one day.

He shrugged and said, "Sure, why not?" like it was no big deal, then sat down at the table across from me. He kept looking my way like he was really pleased about something or else thought I was kind of funny looking.

"I'm Cammie," I said, hoping if I said something he'd stop staring. I was used to people looking at me, stopping what they were doing just to stand back and gawk. People used to watch me down at Mae Cushion's store when I laid my nickel on the counter like they couldn't believe I had enough good sense to pay for the candy I had in my hand. When you live in a small place like Tanner, population 206, it doesn't take much for other people to want to stand back and stare. Only I didn't get any say in the matter. No one consulted me. Maybe God thought he was being funny when he gave me a set of tiny little eyes, or maybe, just maybe, God needed me to have tough skin is all.

I decided I didn't like the way Ed was sitting there smiling at me. I really wanted to make a face at him. If I had thought it would make him stop staring I would have. Instead, I changed the subject and asked Aunt Millie for some paper and a pen.

"You don't need any of that," she snorted, but then Ed smooth-talked her into letting me use her good pen. He made her scrounge around until she found some brown paper that had been wrapped around a parcel she'd got in the mail last week. When someone goes out of their way to try and make you happy, they can't be all that bad. He had a nice-enough-shaped head and I couldn't make out any missing teeth in his smile. His coal-black hair kind of made him look different, but I'm the last one to care about different. Aunt Millie and I both have blonde hair, mine from birth, hers from hydrogen peroxide. At least Ed was paying attention to me, which is more than I could say about Aunt Millie's other boyfriends.

"Let me see what you're doing there," said Ed, pulling the paper away from me. I waited for him to start laughing. Instead he nodded and said, "You've got some pretty nice-looking loops there, Cammie."

"It's writing," I informed him. My marks were crude, but he should have known what it was right away.

"Of course it is. There's lots of loops in writing," he said. "Here, let me show you how to write your name." He put some letters on my sheet of brown paper and passed it over for me to inspect. I held it up close. It was the first time I'd seen my name written out like that. I started right in working to make my letters as smooth as Ed's, but it wasn't as easy as it looked.

"How are *you* going to get to school? Tell me that, 'cause I won't be walking you there every day," Aunt Millie said. I don't think she liked Ed showing me how to write.

"I've got two feet. I can walk," I answered, brave at the

thought of walking there all on my own, something I'd never done before. The school wasn't that far away. I'd been dreaming it in my head, planning out the way to the schoolhouse so I'd be ready when the time came.

Me, just a-strutting down the road without a single care in the world, toting my books and lunch kettle in my hands, walking along like I've got just as much business going to school as the next person, one foot in front of the other, out to the end of the Lake Ridge Road and make a right turn instead of a left like when we go to Mae Cushion's. A piece of cake by my calculations.

"Oh, you've got two feet, do you?" Aunt Millie mocked as she moved her head from one side to the other. My face burned. How could she make fun of me like that in front of Ed Hanover, someone I didn't even know?

"What if you end up getting lost? Besides, you wouldn't be able to copy things off the blackboard," Aunt Millie said as she fiddled with the teapot lid. "Have you thought about that, Miss Smartypants?"

As soon as Ed piped up and said, "School might not be a bad idea, Millie," the little bird inside me made a happy chirp. I gave a quick gasp. I wanted to throw my arms around Ed's scrawny neck and smother him with kisses. I'd never had anyone take my side before. No one was brave enough to go against Aunt Millie.

"Cammie'll go when I think she's ready, and not one day before," sputtered Aunt Millie. It didn't look as though Ed was going to change her mind.

"How old are you, honey?" Ed asked, looking over at me. I could tell he wasn't about to give up without a fight. I was glad to have him in my corner at least.

"Almost ten and three quarters," I said, stealing a look at Aunt Millie. That sounded better than just saying ten, a hint to Aunt Millie that I wasn't getting any younger. Life was already passing me by.

"I already know where you're going with this, Ed, and you can forget it," she said, folding her arms across her chest. A picture of me heading to the outhouse with Aunt Millie's chamber pail swinging at the end of my arm sent whatever hope that was inside me spiralling into the dust. I was doomed.

"How's she going to keep up with the other kids? Look at her. She can barely see what's written on that paper I gave her."

"I can *too* see it," I howled. Just because I have to look really close to see small things doesn't mean I can't see them as good as everyone else. So what if things off in the distance look fuzzy? It's not as if I can't get myself around. I've been doing it my entire life. It used to give Aunt Millie the willies the way I could tell what she was doing from all the way across the room. There's a trick to it that I learned when I was little. You've got to perk your ears just so. You've got to listen for the sound in her voice and the way she holds her head. When your eyes can't see so good your brain makes up the difference, filling in the details as best it can. Even if you're not one hundred percent accurate, no one's ever going to know. But I wasn't about to make mention about any of that to Aunt Millie.

Ed cleared his throat. "Can't the teacher help her? That's what she gets paid for."

Of course the teacher could help me! I'd only known Ed a few minutes and already I could tell he was a genius. The room went silent for a few seconds. Surely Aunt Millie would see the light and change her mind. Ed's words swung like a loose hinge in the air until the teacups clattered against the saucers when Aunt Mille set them down on the kitchen table.

"I don't want to hear any more about this. Do you hear me, the both of you? Ed, you've got no business butting in. Cammie's my responsibility. Remember? So you can keep your two cents to yourself."

Another moment of silence followed. All I was to her was a responsibility, someone for her to feed and water, like a dog tied out back, at least until my mother returned. As if that was ever going to happen.

"Guess who just told *us* off, Cammie?" Ed said, rubbing at the back of his neck.

That was it. I was done for. With my luck, Aunt Millie would live to be a hundred. I'd be stuck in Tanner all my days. Mae Cushion as good as said so. You don't get anywhere these days without going to school. How would I ever get away if I couldn't read or write?

That little bird inside my chest made a feeble chirp before falling to the bottom of its cage. It lay there, flicking its wings back and forth. I held back my tears. The back of my throat burned.

"So Ed, how's it feel to be back in Tanner after all these years?" Aunt Millie poured out tea and started chatting away like a chipmunk. How could she sound chipper when the bottom had just dropped out of my world?

I should have known better than to get my hopes up. Aunt Millie didn't care if I learned anything so long as she gave me a roof over my head and I did what she asked. Who cared if I lived in ignorance all the days of my life? No one, that's who!

A huge ball of anger began to sprout inside me, burning and pulsing with each beat of my heart. I wanted to grab Aunt Millie's voice and rip it through the middle, let her know what it felt like to have your words mean nothing.

I grabbed her pen off the table and scribbled over my beautiful writing, over the place where Ed had just written my name. I scratched the pen into the paper over and over until I'd made a hole. When I was done I threw the pen to the floor at Aunt Millie's feet and ran from the kitchen like the house was on fire.

Chapter Two

"Who's up for another round of drinks?" squealed Aunt Millie. "Saturday night only comes once a week, you know."

Just as the words left her mouth, the sound of money hitting the floor caught my attention. The coins spilled out of Lyle Peterson's clumsy fingers while he was fumbling for change. A few odd pieces of silver were spinning around and around. I dove under the kitchen table without a moment to spare. Seconds after I caught hold of a bright, shiny coin, Aunt Millie grabbed me by the ankles and hauled me backwards across the kitchen floor. At first I laughed, it was kind of fun, until my head flopped forward and my face smacked into the floor. It smarted like a dozen bees all stinging me at once.

"Keep your grubby fingers off Lyle's money," Aunt Millie said, indignant like she wouldn't shortchange him if she thought she could get away with it. I knew Lyle wasn't about to bend over and pick it up. As a matter of fact, Aunt Millie's usually down on the floor scrounging for any loose change herself. The more people sitting around the kitchen on a Saturday night, the more likely she is to find a few stray coins in the morning.

Everyone in the kitchen laughed and hooted like we were part of some sideshow at the exhibition. Aunt Millie was laughing the hardest, her head thrown back like a loon trilling in a windstorm. I'd seen her tip a glass back a few times during the evening. She wouldn't have been laughing so hard if she hadn't been drinking, even I knew that. I jumped to my feet and turned to face her.

"Why, you're no better than that old penny-pincher, Herman Deveau!" she cried out. That brought even more laughter from the crew sitting around the kitchen. My grandfather's stingy ways were well talked about in these parts even though he was rolling in his grave before I was born. They say your reputation follows you all your life, but if you ask me it does more than that. It sticks to you the way a rancid fart sticks to the seat of your pants. It never lets go. Not even once you're dead and gone.

I flung the coin in Aunt Millie's direction. Spite carried it across the kitchen for me. *Take that for laughing at me*, I wanted to cry, *and for not letting me go to school when I've been begging to go for a whole month now.* The coin was full of power when it hit the window directly behind Lyle, and it made a sound like the crack from a gun. The glass broke into tiny pieces and spilled onto the floor. Lyle hopped out of his chair like he'd been sitting on a hot potato. It was probably the fastest he'd moved his whole life.

The kitchen quieted to a hush. If a feather had drifted down and hit the floor, someone would have heard. An awkward tension circled the kitchen waiting for something to take place. It lasted for only half a minute before Aunt Millie started stringing out a whole bunch of curse words.

She made a lunge toward me. Like a weasel I darted out of her reach. I could sense where I needed to go, could feel the objects in my way even before I saw them. I didn't wait around to find out what was going to happen. I ran for the safety of my bedroom. I knew I could make it if I was fast enough, if I didn't think about the fact that I couldn't see so well. If I let my feet lead the way, the rest of me would follow.

Aunt Millie chased me to the bottom of the stairs. My bare feet slapped against the steps. Anger and fear bubbled inside me. With lightning speed she followed me up the stairs, gasping like a sweaty old horse with the heaves.

"Now you stay in your bed, Cammie Deveau. Do you hear me?" Aunt Millie said, forcing the words out of her lungs. I dove for my bed.

"But there's company downstairs!" I cried from beneath a bulging ball of blankets and sheets.

"That's not company. What's downstairs are customers. Do you hear me? Customers. And no place for the likes of you, Cammie Deveau." Aunt Millie closed my bedroom door.

"Some fine place this is," I mumbled. The door swung open the second the words left my lips.

"Just remember, you were born in the back seat of an old Model T, Cammie Deveau. You're no one special. Don't think you are. I didn't have to take you in. Do you think anyone else would have?" She slammed the door shut and left me trembling in the dark. I couldn't fall asleep after all that.

Don't let Aunt Millie's words get the best of you, Cammie. There's plenty of people out there who'd be happy to have you, I whispered in my head. Most times I was able to lift my spirit that way, but that time I couldn't convince myself that it was true. Ed would have stood up for me. He did before, that day in the kitchen when Aunt Millie said I couldn't go to school. Not that it helped, but still it made me feel kind of good at the time. It's fine to tell yourself that you're worth something, but sometimes you need to hear the words come from someone else's mouth.

—

I was born in 1939, the year the Second World War got underway. According to Aunt Millie that wasn't the only war that broke out that year. She claimed folks could hear the rumpus all the way into New Ross the day my mother came home and announced that she was going to have me.

"You caused quite a racket. Both sides of the family put up their dukes. Your father had to join the army and your mother went away. Neither one of them ever came back."

For a lot of years that was all I was told about my mother and father. When it suited her, Aunt Millie could be as tight-lipped as a priest. The more I pried, the tighter those lips became. Aunt Millie's scant version of events wasn't enough to satisfy my baby finger, let alone the burning hunger that was gnawing away in my belly. I wanted to know exactly what *she* said, and then what *he* said, and what were my grandmother's exact words. Did my mother break down and cry? Or did she run off slamming doors and rattling windows?

Details. I used to cry to Aunt Millie, "I want to know the details!"

Sometimes she'd give in then and start talking.

"Now, I'm only going by what was said to me by your mother," Aunt Millie would say. Each time she told the story it would be a little different, but I didn't care. I'd picture it all in my head just the same. Little by little I'd lay all the pieces of my life into one big pile, and on days when I was feeling sad I'd spread them out to admire. Sometimes I'd even make up a few of those details myself. What harm was there in me pretending too? The only ones who could possibly know what was really said would be my mother and my grandmother, and it's hard to say if they would remember after all this time. Memories have a way of wasting away to nothing. All the bumps and bruises get healed over. It's like years down the road it doesn't matter what was said or how it was said; the rest of us are just living with the leftovers.

The plans had all been made. I was supposed to be adopted by some couple in the city, never to be thought of by my parents again. Snap! Just like that I'd disappear from their lives for good. My mother would dust off her hands and go on her way, get married and start popping out a family, without her husband ever knowing the truth. When you're the family secret, no one wants your bones rattling in their closet.

I try not to blame my mother for dumping me out at Aunt Millie's when the adoption fell through. She was barely seventeen when I came on the scene. I try to put myself in her place. Maybe I would have done the same thing. Then I get to thinking that I would at least come to visit my own kid once in a while, and the spite starts building in me. I stop being so understanding, and start flinging things at my bedroom door.

"Why doesn't she ever come?" I whined one day.

"Don't you worry. Your mother's off making her mark. Some day when you're not expecting it, she'll show up right out of the blue."

Aunt Millie would have complained about anyone else taking off like that. You can only excuse so much, even when it comes to family. It's not like Aunt Millie to be so understanding. Who knows, maybe blood really is thicker than water, but wouldn't you think she'd expect her own sister to swing by once in a dog's age just to check on me? It's hard to see your way into someone else's head. Sometimes I wish I could.

My father's side of the family was rich until the stock market crashed and they lost every last cent. By the time I was born the money was just starting to roll back in. Being as poor as church mice all those years didn't stop them from sticking their noses in the air when the rest of the world passed them by. I can only imagine what was going through their heads when they found out I was in the works. I liked Aunt Millie's rendition of events, even though I knew she exaggerated most everything she said, because even a fairy tale, wrapped up in fantasy and magic, is better than knowing nothing about your life.

"That highfaluting grandmother of yours put her foot down. Couldn't have some scandal like that dirtying up the family name. The Deveaus were high society, don't you think they weren't. The king and queen of Sheppard Square. She couldn't admit that her Charlie was less than perfect."

It was best not to interrupt when Aunt Millie got on a rant about my grandmother. Funny how things can change like the flip of a coin. When they were younger, Aunt Millie and my grandmother were the best of friends. Wherever one went, the other followed. They wore one another's clothes and dolled each other up for the Saturday night dances.

"We had our age difference, some twenty odd years," said Aunt Millie, "but you'd never know it to see us together. Sophia was one for having fun back in those days."

But time pulled them apart, according to Aunt Millie.

"The money got the best of her, made her act all high-class and surly. Not that Herman wouldn't have had a hand in that. Funny how some people can be influenced by others. I finally had enough of her actions and called our friendship quits. I'll tell you one thing, if I'd known what was going to happen down the line, I'd never have given that old battleaxe the time of day."

My grandmother turning my mother away just seemed like the icing on the cake.

"She wasn't about to take in some young thing with a

child, seeing how there was no real proof that her Charlie was the father." Aunt Millie's voice always took on a snotty tone whenever she mentioned my father's side of the family. She'd tilt her head from side to side to show how uppity she thought they were. Too bad my father went off and got himself killed in the war. There was no way for anyone to prove whose kid I really was. All I had was Aunt Millie's word on that.

One particular day, Aunt Millie saw my grandmother, her once-upon-a-time best friend, coming out of the dry goods store in Sheppard Square.

"Why, there's the old battleaxe herself," Aunt Millie mumbled. I felt her body tense, her hand tightened around mine. I knew, without being told, the old battleaxe heading our way was my grandmother. I pushed back my shoulders. I prepared myself in case my grandmother spoke to me. I had thought about this moment often, always knowing there was a possibility our paths would one day cross. Sheppard Square isn't all that big, and it's the only place the folks in Tanner have to do their shopping.

She hurried past us that day without giving a sideways glance. I stopped in my tracks and looked back. Her navy blue dress waved goodbye to me in the breeze. There went my real life. The one I should have had.

"I'm Cammie Deveau," I yelled, but she kept on walking.

"Come on, Cammie," Aunt Mille said, tugging fast to my arm. "She's not worth wasting your time on."

Sounds drifted upward from the kitchen below, making it impossible for me to sleep. Aunt Millie's laughter was the worst of all. It sent tiny prickles up my spine. I tossed and turned. I swallowed tears. I wiped my snotty nose into my pillow. A long sliver of moonlight came though my window and fell across the foot of my bed, looking like a silver sword. I wiped my tears and sat up.

Me, picking the sword up off the bed, brave heart beating in my chest. I run downstairs swinging it high above my head. Aunt Millie ducks for cover; the men take one look at me and hurry for the door. I'm yelling "Get moving, suckers!" Aunt Millie is cowering in the corner. I point my sword at her. She makes a squeak and runs for the door. When they're all gone and the kitchen is empty, I march back upstairs, lay my sword across the foot of my bed, and go to sleep.

Dreaming up a way to get back at them all made me feel better for a little while, but then I was back to feeling the hurt all over again. When the voices below in the kitchen trickled away to nothing, I rolled over and looked out the window. My moonbeam was gone. There was nothing but black out there, an unknown question waiting for an answer. Too bad, but I was all out of answers. Some days nothing in my life seemed to make any sense.

Chapter Three

A few weeks later we headed off to the schoolhouse bright and early. There was a pinch-your-nose kind of smell in the air that morning, and it kept getting stronger the closer we came to the Merry farm. I held my breath, but the stench wiggled between my clenched teeth and made me want to gag. The air was heavy, a dampness left over from the big rain we'd had the night before. Aunt Millie made me put on a rain bonnet, like the one she was wearing, and I felt stupid. What would the other kids think? I was sure none of them would be wearing one.

The brim of the bonnet kept rutching down across my eyes. I'd stop every now and again to push it back in place. A light drizzle was coming down. It was supposed to clear later on in the day, or so Aunt Millie said. She'd rattled on about all sorts of things that morning while she fixed me breakfast: the weather, the ingrown toenail on her left foot, the fact that she was nearly out of oatmeal and would have to head off to Mae Cushion's after she got me enrolled in school to get some more.

"The teacher's name is Miss Muise," she'd said. "I've been asking around about her."

Who would Aunt Millie ask about the schoolteacher, one of the Saturday-night regulars who came to the house to buy moonshine? I wanted to laugh. She continued to talk away while slicing bread and spreading a thin layer of honey on it for my lunch, waving the knife in the air as she spoke. It was one of those ordinary family moments I always figured the rest of the world had, but for me they were as scarce as hen's teeth. I sat at the table eating the oatmeal she'd made me, thinking how I'd like to wrap this morning up and keep it with me all the time.

I was doing my best to keep up to Aunt Millie, who was hoofing it along like nobody's business. The road was dotted with potholes that were filled with brown, muddy water deep enough to get your foot wet. Aunt Millie steered me around the holes as best and as fast as she could.

"You get your good socks dirty and you'll know it," she said.

The Merrys' barn was off in the distance. It was big and red—a dull kind of red that made me hope it would disappear into thin air and take its nasty odour with it.

"Stupid pigs!" Aunt Millie sputtered as she increased her stride.

"That's cow manure," I said, stopping to pull back my rain bonnet. Everyone in Tanner knew that Jim Merry kept cattle. She whirled around to face me, stopping suddenly in the middle of the road.

"Don't start in on me, Cammie," she said, wagging her finger. "I'm not in the best of moods, and I won't be held responsible if you end up with a slap upside the head. Now, you've been warned."

She straightened her shoulders and started back down the road lickety-split. I wasn't scared of the slaps she threatened me with. I'd learned a long time ago that the ones to watch out for came without warning, usually once she had a few drinks in her.

I couldn't help but wonder what Aunt Millie was going to say to the teacher once we got to the schoolhouse. I'd been begging to go ever since I'd heard Mae Cushion discussing my future at the beginning of summer. Aunt Millie hadn't wanted to hear about it. But then suddenly she wanted me to get an education.

"Just because you're half-blind doesn't mean you can't be learning to read and write like the rest of them," Aunt Millie had said a week before. I could hardly believe my good luck. It's too bad it was only happening because Drew

Bordmann came into our lives a few weeks back. Seemed like every time I turned around he was waltzing through the door. He hardly even bothered to talk to me. I don't suppose he ever did a full day's work, seeing as how his father owned the big sawmill in Sheppard's Square. Must be nice being the boss's son, coming and going as you please. I figured it was only a matter of time before he moved in for good.

This talk about school didn't start until I caught them in the bedroom one day in the middle of the afternoon. I could hear Aunt Millie giggling and whispering. I banged on the door with my fist. I yelled for her to come out. I didn't want to be down in the kitchen all by myself. The plate of cookies she'd left for me was just about gone. I didn't like the loneliness and quiet.

Drew came barging out and ordered me to get lost. Aunt Millie stuck her head out the crack of the door and told me to find something to do. I went off to my room and started looking through the *Standard* magazines. I looked at the photos of the king and the queen gallivanting all over the countryside just months before the war broke out. Usually the pictures cheered me up, but that day they didn't. I looked at their smiling faces, at the people standing there waving to them as they drove by. What I wouldn't do to trade places with them for even one day—but who in their right mind would want to trade places with me?

—

I could hear barking before we even reached the Merry farm. Like the smell of manure in the air that morning, their dog couldn't wait for us to get there either.

"Don't look in," Aunt Millie said before we reached the Merrys' mailbox at the end of their drive. She pulled on my arm. "Just keep walking."

"But he's usually tied," I said.

"I'm not worried about that dog," she said with a scaly laugh.

A man yelled out for the dog to shut up. It whinged like someone had stepped on its tail. After that it didn't bark anymore.

"I don't want you near Jim Merry's kid. No playing at school, no walking home together, no nothing. Do you hear me on that, Cammie Deveau? That man is mean through and through. Nothing but a lowlife, he is, and that boy won't grow up to know any better."

I knew Jim Merry came to the house for moonshine, but since I didn't even know his kid I didn't mind promising to stay away from him if it meant I could go to school. It sounded like a good enough deal to me. I turned my head and peeked in when we walked past the driveway. I could make out a darkish figure walking toward the barn, but I couldn't tell much from that distance. It might have been Jim Merry or it might have been his wife or maybe it was that son of his, the one I wasn't supposed to talk to. I didn't even know his name.

I called out for Aunt Millie to slow down, but she didn't let on she heard. She kept going like the schoolhouse was on fire and she wanted to be the one to throw the first bucket of water. It wasn't hard to sense that Aunt Millie was uptight. I wouldn't have thought it, not the way she could make herself sound real tough when there was someone standing outside the door late at night. Then again, of all the things I might have imagined her doing, I never once pictured her entering the Tanner schoolhouse for anything.

"I want to get there before the teacher rings the bell. I don't want everyone listening to what I've got to say," said Aunt Millie just as the schoolhouse came into sight. It was a brighter red than the Merry barn, and not nearly as big as I'd imagined, but I didn't care. I made my feet go even faster.

"I'll have to put Turple down for your last name," continued Aunt Millie. "I don't want that old battleaxe over in Sheppard Square making trouble for you. Besides, Deveau isn't on your birth certificate."

I was almost too excited to care what Aunt Millie planned on saying once we got there. Would the teacher tell me I could stay? Would she tell me my eyesight was too poor? Would she laugh at me and tell me to go home? All those questions were flipping and flopping inside me.

"Let's get this over with," said Aunt Millie, taking a big breath. My arm felt as though it was being yanked from the socket when she pulled on it. I stubbed my toe on a rock in the road, catching myself moments before hitting the dirt. "Jeez, Cammie, don't be so clumsy. Must I watch you all the time?" she said as she continued her pace.

Chapter Four

"I want Cammie registered for school," said Aunt Millie, tapping her finger on the teacher's desk. Her voice echoed inside the walls of the schoolhouse. "We missed out last year because the other teacher refused to teach her, but Cammie's got as much right to learn as the rest of them here."

That was the first lie out of Aunt Millie's mouth. I wondered how many more were to follow.

"The school year has already started," the teacher said. She sounded doubtful. "You should have registered her the first of September."

"School just started two weeks ago, so I'm registering her now. What can you learn in two weeks, anyway?" Aunt Millie snapped. I stood, waiting for the longest pause on record to be broken. I was sure the teacher's face turned pink.

"You said there's a problem with her eyesight?" The teacher looked directly at me. I hadn't taken my eyes off her since we walked through the door. If I looked pitiful and sad, maybe she'd say yes.

"Cammie can see good enough when she wants to. It's not like she can't do chores and things like that," Aunt Millie said.

"Chores are one thing, but what about seeing to read and write?"

"If I get in close I can see small things real good," I piped in, knowing that if I had to rely on Aunt Millie to explain things for me I'd be doomed.

"That's good, Cammie, but what about the blackboard? Can you see what's written there?" The teacher pointed behind her. I peeled my eyes away from her face. I knew better than to even look. I thought I could see some faint white lines here and there, but that was about it. If I couldn't make out the writing on the blackboard while I was standing near the front of the room, I for sure wouldn't see anything once I was sitting at one of the desks. I shook my head. I knew I shouldn't lie. Lying was Aunt Millie's department, and something I didn't have a whole lot of practise doing. The teacher would see right through me.

When a few kids walked into the school while Aunt Millie and the teacher were hashing things out, Aunt Millie looked at them and told them to scram.

"We're talking business here," she snapped. They ran

outdoors like they'd been scared by a goblin. They stood just outside the schoolhouse with the door wide open.

"Don't go in the schoolhouse," one girl shouted. "Millie Turple's in there with that blind girl of hers." A chorus of laughter echoed across the breeze.

"I'll kindly thank you not to speak to the children in that manner, Mrs. Turple. Must I remind you that I'm in charge? I give the orders in here," stated Miss Muise.

Aunt Millie waved her hand in the air and continued to babble away as if she hadn't heard. "Everyone has a right to learn," she said, "even Cammie here. Why, just because she was born this way doesn't mean she shouldn't be given the same advantage as the other children. We can't all be born perfect, now can we, Miss Muise?

There, just you wait, Aunt Millie is going to ruin this for me if she doesn't keep quiet, I thought.

"I couldn't do a thing with the teacher last year, hard as I tried," Aunt Millie lied, "but I was hoping somehow you'd be different, being as how you're new to these parts and all." Finally she stopped clacking away long enough to give the teacher a chance to speak. Miss Muise took a deep breath.

"I will allow Cammie to stay," she said quietly after a brief silence.

"See there, Cammie, didn't I tell you I'd make this right if you let me do the talking?" Aunt Millie was puffed out as big as a bullfrog.

Miss Muise cleared her throat and continued. "I will allow Cammie to stay. Not because of you, Mrs. Turple, but because I'd never turn away any child who wants to learn."

That let the air out of Aunt Millie and the smile slid off her face. She stood looking Miss Muise over like she was considering whether or not to leave good enough alone. I knew there was something she was itching to say. There always was. That mouth of hers had stirred up plenty of trouble in the past. I wasn't going to let her start a racket here at the schoolhouse. I nudged Aunt Millie with my elbow.

"Aren't you going to Mae Cushion's this morning?" I reminded her quickly.

For a wonder, she turned without saying another word and stomped her way out the door. The moment her foot hit the ground outside, some of the choicest words you'd ever want to hear shot out of Aunt Millie's mouth. I thought I was going to pass out. When she was through, she turned back toward the schoolhouse.

"And that's *Miss* Turple, for your information. You might be the boss in that measly little schoolhouse," she grumbled, "but you're not the boss of the whole outdoors, and you're not the boss of me."

When the schoolhouse finally filled up, Miss Muise led me to a seat at the front of the classroom so that I could be close to the blackboard.

"Cammie, I want you to sit beside Evelyn," said Miss Muise sharply, getting everyone's attention. It wasn't much different from being gawked at down at Mae Cushion's store; you'd think I'd have felt right at home.

But I had so much to get used to—these people, the school, the things in the school—and to top it all off I couldn't be Cammie Deveau anymore. Cammie Turple sounded all wrong. I wiggled in my seat as Evelyn came toward me. Her shirt was the oddest shade of green I'd ever seen. I knew I wouldn't have any trouble recognizing her from a distance. I hoped she wasn't one of the girls who'd stood outside the schoolhouse laughing at Aunt Millie earlier.

When Miss Muise said, "Evelyn Merry, I'd like you to be Cammie's helper for the year," I nearly fell off my chair. Merry? Evelyn Merry? It couldn't be. But as soon as Evelyn sat down at the double desk beside me, I knew for a fact he was that boy Aunt Millie had warned me to stay away I tried not to smile too big. When you're stuck with a name like that people are bound to make fun.

He looked over at me and whispered, "Do you like cows?" so loud I thought everyone must have heard. I wondered if he knew about the faint odour of cow manure on his clothes. I was glad it wasn't as overpowering as the smell outside his barn had been that morning.

"I sure do," I said. I wasn't about to tell him what I really thought about his stinky old cows. If Jim Merry had a bad temper, maybe his boy did too.

"Someday I'm going to have a sloop ox of my own. Pa even said so." He squirmed in his seat with his hands folded on the desk. He looked at me and grinned. I don't even think he noticed my little eyes.

—

At lunchtime the other kids gathered near the swings and handed their best whispers amongst themselves. I could see them chasing each other around the big trees, laughing like it was the biggest fun in the world. I sat on the grass and watched them play, waiting to be asked to join in.

When someone called out "Blind-eyed Cammie!" everyone giggled. I considered running off to find Miss Muise, reporting their actions to her, but what if it only made matters worse? There were more of them than there was of me. What chance would I stand? I grew up knowing I looked different from everyone else, not to mention my poor eyesight always setting me apart, but no one ever dared make fun of me because of it. Aunt Millie would have put them in their place right smartly.

"Just because you started out at the rotten end of things,

Cammie, doesn't mean you should settle for less than the rest of us. Now, hold your head up high and don't pay any attention," she'd say if someone made a rude remark about me when we were in town. She'd make sure she said it loud enough for everyone to hear. The funny thing about Aunt Millie was, she could say all the mean things she wanted to me, but let someone else say something mean and she'd jump right in to my rescue.

I looked quickly to my right and saw the same green shirt I'd sat beside all morning. Next thing I knew it was heading my way.

"Want to play cat's cradle?" asked Evelyn, stopping directly in front of me.

"I don't know how," I said, trying to ignore one more outburst of laughter coming from the other side of the schoolyard.

"I'll show you," he said, in the face of their laughter, as he wrapped the string around my hands. I held it up close to see while he showed me what to do, guiding my fingers into the spaces. He didn't even snap at me when I got the string tangled up. He just laughed and said, "You'll get the hang of it after a while."

I looked over at Evelyn, at his thick mop of brown hair, and smiled. I had no idea why Aunt Millie had told me to stay away from the Merry boy when he was the only one in school who would talk to me. He seemed like an ordinary kind of boy. No outstanding features, no horrible birthmarks or hideous deformities that I could make out. The best part was the way he treated me like a regular, everyday person. He didn't even care that I had bad eyesight.

A voice cried out, "Evelyn!" and the laughter started up again. A whisker of shame brushed up against me. Was I no better than the rest of them? When Miss Muise had called Evelyn by name I had wanted to laugh myself. It was such a strange name for a boy. What had his parents been thinking?

"You'll get used to them making fun after a while," said Evelyn Merry as he wrapped the string around my hands again. "I don't even hear them anymore."

—

I could hardly wait to tell Aunt Millie about all the things I'd done my first day at school. I wanted to show her the picture I had drawn with the crayons Miss Muise kept in her desk drawer, and tell her I wanted a pack of my very own. Green and blue and red were spread across the paper. I was sure I'd never seen anything so pretty.

"Creativity is food for the soul," Miss Muise had said. "Express your creativity on the page, Cammie. It's something we must all do. We must find that spark of creativity and nurture it until it becomes a flaming fire."

I could hear someone snicker but I didn't care. I hung

on Miss Muise's words, eager to hear more. That little bird inside me spread its wings out wide. It flew high, it flew low, it flew forward and back. It tickled me and made me vibrate with happiness. No one had ever told me that creativity existed. Until I'd met Miss Muise I hadn't heard of it. I was convinced that was the reason I'd scarcely been able to eat a bite at lunch. I was now filled with creativity, a delicious, wonderful-tasting thing. I wanted to draw and colour every spare moment I had.

"That's not too bad," Aunt Millie said, looking over my creativity, the food that had filled my soul all day. "If you could see like the rest of us, it might even be good."

I was suddenly famished. I should have forced myself to eat the bread and honey Aunt Millie had packed. I should have known better. I shouldn't have been so foolish as to let creativity be my only food for the day. Who was I to be drawing pictures and putting pretty colours onto paper? I grabbed the picture away from Aunt Millie and squished into a tight ball.

"What did you do that for?" she asked. Taking the balled-up picture from me, she straightened it out. She looked at it closely from all angles. "Whatever happened to good old reading, writing, and 'rithmetic? Miss Muise has it pretty darn easy, if you ask me."

Chapter Five

By the time October came I started to feel as though I was meant for school life, certainly more than the bootlegging life I had with Aunt Millie. Not that the kids at school would give me the time of day, but at least I was fitting into a regular kind of life like everyone else. I listened to everything Miss Muise had to say, knowing I would have to work extra hard if I wanted to get caught up to everyone else. I wasn't going to let the fact that I hadn't been going to school all along stop me. Lamenting about the tough breaks we're handed doesn't change a thing. I still had plans of trading that old life of mine for something better, and I knew it was going to take a lot of work. I can't say the kids' teasing didn't get to me every now and again, but Evelyn always had a way of turning things around. The best part was, if I tried real hard, I could forget who I was, at least for a little time during the day.

—

"What am I doing now?"

"Sticking out your tongue."

Evelyn's arms flopped down by his side. He thought he'd tricked me that time.

"How do you know?" he asked. He was impressed. I could hear it in his voice.

"I can see something pink where your mouth is. What else would it be?"

Just like everyone else, I can put two and two together. Not that I don't get confused by times, because I do. But I can usually do a decent job of covering it up when I have to.

Evelyn began testing me as soon as we started out to the river that day, thinking up things for me to look at, wondering exactly how much I could see, trying to figure me out. All I had on my mind was learning to swim.

"So how come you've got to get in close to read and write?" he asked. I liked that he didn't tiptoe around the subject the way most people do. It's not like I've got some contagious disease.

"How should I know? I came this way. It's not like I made up the rules."

I was glad he laughed when I said that. Sometimes I can't stop myself from sounding like Aunt Millie. I say something that comes out snotty and I wish I could take it back. Too late once it's out there in the open.

I wonder if my mother has a sharp tongue in her head or if Aunt Millie was rubbing off on me? Maybe it's one of those things that gets passed on down like a family heirloom. Except this isn't something to get excited about, like crystal or fine china. All the ways to make me want to rip out my hair are at the tip of Aunt Millie's tongue, just waiting to be said. I don't think she can help herself.

When your tongue is sharp, people think the rest of you must be too. As mean as Aunt Millie seems, she wouldn't be letting me live with her if she was all bad. Even Aunt Millie has her good spells. She says I should count my lucky stars that I'm not sitting on the doorstep of an orphan house somewhere. Knowing all that doesn't stop me from getting riled at her, though; doesn't stop me from wishing those good spells of hers weren't so few and far between.

—

Can't say that I was fussy about this game of Evelyn's. After the first few times it got to be downright boring. I knew the kids at school made faces at me. It doesn't take smarts to figure that out. I made sure not to let my brain fill in any of the details, though. I made myself skim over it all.

"Who do they think they are?" grunted Aunt Millie when I complained to her the first time. "The women around Tanner might think they're ladies, but if they had an ounce of good manners they would have taught some to their own kids." Aunt Millie never had much use for the women around these parts. I think the feeling was mutual, seeing as how none of them ever stopped in to visit.

When Evelyn started doing crazy things like crossing his eyes and stretching his mouth out with his fingers, moving a little farther back each time he made a new face, I started to get a teensy bit peeved. I wanted to get down to business, get this whole thing underway. Aunt Millie had gone into Sheppard Square with Drew. I could count on her being gone for a good three hours or more. No one ever rushed Aunt Millie when she was doing the town, not even Drew Bordmann. But would three hours be enough?

I quickly reminded Evelyn why we'd come to the river. The time for games was over. We had discovered a small clearing on the riverbank a few weeks back. Not far from it, some fir trees grew close to one another with their branches tangled and matted together. Once Evelyn found a way into the thicket, we knew it was the perfect place for a secret camp. It was even big enough to stand up in once we were inside. Best of all, no one would ever think to look for us there. Evelyn's pa was too mean to come looking for him, and all Aunt Millie thought about was spending time with Drew. Could be Evelyn and me were making up for lost time in the friendship department. Whenever we could, we'd spend every spare moment together. Who would have thought that having a friend could be so much fun?

We decorated the inside of the camp with some coloured bottles we'd dug out of the ground up near the stone wall on Millie's property. Dark blue *Evening of Paris* bottles and some empty cold-cream jars were lined up on an old board near the doorway. In the beginning, Evelyn thought it looked too girlish, but when I showed up one day with two *Red Liniment* bottles he stopped complaining. Evelyn placed them just so on the board.

Ideas are like soap bubbles. They shimmer and shine when the light hits them just right. I'm not sure who got the idea in the first place. When it comes right down to it, it hardly matters. The river's nice and wide. Not far up from the camp we made is the perfect place for swimming. Evelyn was more than set to teach me how.

"Everyone in Tanner knows how to swim," he said. "Everyone and his dog."

It was Thanksgiving weekend. Warm enough to make most people in Tanner declare it felt more like summer than fall. And warm enough for me to say that I wasn't about to have some mangy old dog get the better of me. Quickly, I changed into the cut-off pants Evelyn brought for me, a pair he'd outgrown last year. I kept my undershirt on for a top. I wasn't one of those bathing beauties you hear tell of, but I would do. I lowered myself into the water and waited for Evelyn to join me.

"You'll be fine. It's not even over your head down here. I tried," said Evelyn. He showed me the way to move my hands and told me to kick my feet.

At first I was afraid. I couldn't see where I was going. The river may as well have been the Atlantic Ocean, it seemed so big.

I slapped at the water, squealing, "I can't, I can't!" like a sissy.

But Evelyn said, "You can! You can! You don't swim with your eyes."

The moment he said that, something changed inside. If you do something long enough you're bound to get the hang of it, and when someone keeps saying you can, it makes you try all the harder. I practised until my arms and legs felt like jelly. I kicked and paddled and kicked some more. I swallowed water. I coughed. By the time I was ready to head back home I could make it across the narrow part of the river all on my own.

"I did it, Evelyn. I did it!" I was swollen up with pride. The little bird inside me flapped its wings.

"See, Cammie?" said Evelyn, sounding mighty proud himself as we headed for home. "I knew you could do it."

I wanted to run through Tanner and announce the news, scream it out for everyone to hear, let them know this wonderful thing about me. But I knew it would be a waste of time. Not a single soul in Tanner was ever going to care that Blind-eyed Cammie had learned to swim. I knew that for a fact.

I looked over at Evelyn and smiled.

We cared. Both of us. And that was all I needed.

—

Drew's truck was parked around back when I got home. There hadn't been time to change out of my wet clothes at the river. I'd spent too much time learning to swim. If Aunt Millie caught me walking in, wet from head to toe, you can bet I'd have some fancy explaining to do.

Right away, I could hear Aunt Mille and Drew when I came through the front door. I snuck across the floor, careful not to make a sound. They were out in the kitchen rowing about something, but then all of a sudden they stopped. One of the steps squeaked beneath my weight.

"Is that you, Cammie?" Aunt Millie called out. My heart made a big flop. I beat it up the stairs. Aunt Millie's shoes clicked across the living room floor and stopped at the bottom of the stairs. By that time I'd made it to my bedroom.

"Did you hear me, Cammie? What are you up to?"

"I'm just looking through my magazines," I called out,

trying to sound as casual-like as possible. She paused for a few moments. I wondered if she would believe me.

"You know what's the matter with you? You spend too much time in your bedroom, Cammie Deveau," she said, as she clomped back into the kitchen.

Chapter Six

"Pa won't even care if I pass. He'd be happy if I stayed and helped out on the farm," said Evelyn, swinging his report card in his hand. I knew Evelyn would never fail in school. He was far too clever for that.

Right before she gave out our first-term report cards, Miss Muise said we had to have them signed before we brought them back. I was half expecting Aunt Millie to get pigheaded and refuse. Besides, I was willing to bet she wouldn't care what I had for grades.

"I might have to sign it myself if Aunt Millie won't." At least Evelyn's Ma would sign his without a fuss.

"What about bribery?" asked Evelyn.

"Blackmail would be more like it," I said, and we both hooted.

When I thought I heard a sound coming from somewhere up the road, I made for Evelyn to stop laughing.

"Listen," I whispered, grabbing him by the arm. The thing about walking home from school with Evelyn Merry was, I had to keep one ear on the road at all times. If a vehicle came barrelling our way we'd have to act quick. If we carried on too loudly we'd drown out the noises coming our way. No amount of laughter on our part would be worth someone catching us walking home together and telling Aunt Millie. Being a bootlegger, Aunt Millie was Tanner's most famous person. Most everyone landed there at one time or another. It would only be a matter of time before someone ended up tittle-tattling what they'd seen. One thing was in our favour: usually there wasn't a soul out driving during the weekdays, since most everyone who owned a vehicle was either working in the woods or farming. Of course, that also meant Evelyn had to keep his eyes peeled. You never knew when someone might be coming down the road on foot. People have a way of showing up when you're not expecting them to. Good thing Evelyn could see a lot better than me.

I told Evelyn to scram, hoping he could move faster than the vehicle that was headed our way. He jumped down into the ditch.

"Find a tree to hide behind," I said as he scurried into the woods. With most of the leaves gone, I knew the bushes wouldn't make a very good hiding place. You've got to consider all possibilities when trouble's knocking at the door. When a vehicle came up from behind me and slowed down, I sucked in my breath. Was it someone I knew? Probably not, but still... When I caught a glimpse of green metal to my right, I knew right away it was Ed Hanover's truck. It had been over a month since I'd seen him. My guess was Drew Bordmann being at the house probably had something to do with that.

"How's it going, Cammie?" he asked.

"Pretty good," I answered. I was kind of hoping he'd state his business and get going. If I went skimpy on the conversation he might get bored and leave.

"I'm headed your way. Hop in."

Hop in? Great. I had no choice. If I said no it would make him suspicious. Who in their right mind would pass up a ride home? I walked around to the passenger's side and opened the door.

"Does you friend want a ride too?" he asked, his mouth stretched out big.

"My friend?" I said innocently, thinking I could trick Ed by playing dumb.

"The young man hiding behind that tree over there." Ed stuck his head out the window and yelled out for Evelyn to join us. I should have known better.

Evelyn jumped in the truck beside me. "I promised I

wouldn't hang out with Evelyn Merry," I said. "You won't say anything to Aunt Millie, will you?"

"What's the problem with him? He seems like a regular kid to me…Are you a regular kid?" Ed asked, looking across at Evelyn.

"I guess so," said Evelyn, giving a small shrug.

"So you're not going to say anything, right?" I'd been around Ed enough to know he was easygoing. Only sometimes it was hard to make him be serious.

"Do I seem like a snitch to you?"

I shook my head. I had to hope Ed knew how to keep his trap shut, that he understood the seriousness of the situation. I was pretty sure he did.

"What's that you got there?" he asked before taking off down the road.

I looked down at the brown sealed envelope I was holding fast to.

"My first report card."

"How did you do?"

"I didn't look yet." I was dying to know what Miss Muise had written about me. I was waiting until I was in my room before looking. You're best off getting bad news when there's no one around to watch.

"Well, crack her open," Ed urged.

"I can't." I pulled my report card close to my chest. What

if Miss Muise had marked me low? She had said once that I caught on quickly, but it could have been a trick to make everyone else work harder. *If Blind-eyed Cammie can catch on, why can't the rest of you losers?*

"Well, I can," said Ed, pulling it from me. I squirmed as the paper crinkled. I kept quiet while Ed looked it over.

"Says here you're making excellent progress. Well, look at that, Cammie! Excellent progress. And it says you're working real hard and reading at level two. Level two? You're reading already? Well, look at that." Ed let out a whistle and a feeling of glee hiccoughed inside me.

I didn't imagine Aunt Millie would even care what Miss Muise had to say in my report card, seeing as how she thought Miss Muise was wasting our time on things like drawing and embroidery. The grumbling she did the day we went to Mae Cushion's to buy some broadcloth to make potholders wasn't fit to be heard.

"Any nitwit can thread a needle," she'd said.

It wasn't until I told Aunt Millie how nice Miss Muise was that she started finding fault with most everything she did. When I got tired of her grumbling all the time, I stopped telling her what we were doing in school. I could always tell if she and Drew had pulled off another one of their fights. That's when she'd prod me about school, wanting to know this and that. The first few months she and

Drew were all lovey-dovey, but after a while he couldn't do a thing to please her. That's when her spitefulness would start. Then she and Drew broke up and she just wasn't fit to be around.

"In light of this new development, I say we go for an ice cream cone to celebrate. Cammie, are you up for one?" asked Ed.

I squealed out a yes that could have made old man Cleveland jump, and he's near deaf. Mae Cushion had just started selling ice cream last summer and Aunt Millie had been too tight to buy me one. Oh, how I'd been dreaming of having one, letting its sweetness tantalize my tongue. I thought my first ice cream from Mae's would be on a hot July day, not way out in the fall, but I didn't care if I had icicles hanging off me so long as I could have one.

"What say you, Evelyn Merry? You got any place better to be? Want to come for an ice cream with us?" asked Ed.

Evelyn's parents were plenty slack when it came to knowing where he was so long as he was home come chore time. Good thing, too. I'd probably never have learned to swim or even made such good friends with Evelyn otherwise.

"Ice cream," said Evelyn with a quick nod.

"Then it's off to Sheppard Square we go," said Ed, turning right around in the middle of the road, spinning up rocks and dirt.

—

A few minutes earlier and we'd have skinned out of Mae Cushion's store and been on our way home without running smack dab into Aunt Millie. If my vanilla ice cream knew anything at all it would have jumped off the cone and rolled around in the dirt rather than face her. What was she doing at Mae Cushion's store in the middle of the week, anyway?

"What's going on here, Ed?" she demanded, stopping in the doorway. Her head snapped around, and I could tell she had spied my ice cream cone. "Cammie, why aren't you home starting supper?"

Wouldn't that cramp a person, running into her like that, the three of us holding triple-scoop ice cream cones with hardly a lick taken off them?

"A celebration was in order. Today's report card day, and Cammie has a whole slew of Bs to brag about. There's even an A thrown in there too. Pretty darn good for someone just starting this year. She's at reading level two," said Ed with a grin plastered across his face. "Bet you wouldn't have guessed that."

Aunt Millie's face didn't budge an inch. Right now, getting her to crack a smile would be like trying to pry Lyle Peterson away from the kitchen table before twelve o'clock on a Saturday night. There was the grouchiness from the breakup, and to top it off, the law had shown up one day last week. She blamed Drew for reporting her for bootlegging, and maybe he did. They didn't find her stash of moonshine, and you'd think she'd have at least been satisfied about that. I sometimes wondered what it would take to make her happy, at least for more than a few days at a time.

"Can't you find anything better to do, Ed Hanover, than joyride around Sheppard Square on a weekday afternoon?" she snapped. "Let me guess, you quit your job again."

I felt bad for Ed. Aunt Millie had no business pointing out the fact that he had trouble hanging on to a job, especially in front of that old busybody Mae Cushion. I wasn't sure what it would take to get his feathers ruffled, though. He didn't say anything back, not one word, not like most people would. I wouldn't have much blamed him if he had.

I wasn't sure if I should keep eating my ice cream, but not eating it wasn't going to change a thing. I gave it a few good licks before Aunt Millie swatted me in the back of the head. My head snapped forward and a splodge of vanilla ice cream hit my nose. I wiped it away, resisting the urge to holler out and ask her what she did that for.

She looked directly at Evelyn. "What's *he* doing here?" she snapped.

Her words poked hard, like a stiff uppercut to the chin. I was doomed. Being caught in Evelyn Merry's company would take a powerful amount of smooth-talking to fix. I wouldn't even know where to start. I gave Ed a pathetic look. How was I going to wiggle out of this one?

"You can blame me if you want," Ed piped in. "I found this young fellow on the Lake Ridge Road. Figured I might as well ask him to come along too. Why not? The more the merrier, I always say. Would have took the whole school if they'd been on the road." Ed filled his voice with enthusiasm as he stretched the truth out before Aunt Millie.

I'm willing to bet I looked guilty as sin, standing in the doorway hoping above all hope that she would buy his explanation. I felt some ice cream trickle onto my fingers.

"You must have more money than brains, Ed Hanover, or else you're just plain showing off. You don't even know this boy." Before Aunt Millie could say anything more, Ed cut in.

"Name your flavour, Millie Turple. There's vanilla and chocolate and even wild strawberry."

"There's also cherry vanilla," said Mae in the background. For once I was glad the old biddie was butting in.

The idea of Aunt Millie getting her own ice cream won out in the end.

"Strawberry might not be so bad," she said cautiously,

as if she were stepping through cow droppings in her good shoes. Ed turned toward Evelyn and me.

"Jump in the truck and wait for us," he said, giving his ice cream a lick.

Relief knocked at my ribs. I wished I were as good at smooth-talking Aunt Millie as Ed Hanover was.

"Thanks, Ed," I whispered. He tousled my hair. I walked by, licking my ice cream cone like a mad person, trying to eat it as fast as I could. I overheard him offer Aunt Millie a lift home as he headed toward the ice cream freezer. How Ed could butter up Aunt Millie so slick was beyond me.

"I hope you aren't making a mess over everything, Cammie," said Aunt Millie as she opened the truck door with a big old ice cream cone stuck in her fist. She climbed in and slammed the door. I looked over at Evelyn and shrugged—nothing new for Aunt Millie. When your brain is full of snotty comments they're bound to find a way to your mouth.

I wolfed down the rest of my ice cream like it was going out of style. So much for nice and slow. So much for that tantalizing sweetness. All I could think about was getting it gone before Aunt Millie did something more to take away my fun.

Aunt Millie handed over my report card the very next morning.

"You're doing good," she said. "Keep it up."

"Is it signed?"

"On the dotted line. Right where it said parent or guardian." Before I made it out the door she stopped me.

"Cammie," she said.

I could tell something was up by the tone in her voice. Would she expect me to stay home now that Drew wasn't around to keep her company through the day? I'd been expecting her to say something ever since they broke up. Was she finally getting around to it now that she knew how good I was doing in school?

"I don't want to hear tell of you hanging out with that Merry boy again. Do you hear me?"

"But that wasn't my fault," I protested.

"Just see to it you listen or else."

I wasn't much interested in what the "or else" was. Sometimes life with Aunt Millie was just one racket after another, other times it went along smooth as a silk stocking. The only thing was, I could pretty much count on there being a racket sooner or later. You wear a pair of silk stockings long enough, they're bound to get full of runs.

Chapter Seven

Spring has a way of making your heart glad after a long cold winter, but when there's something else tickling away at you it makes you all the more excited.

I raced toward the house with tiny bird wings thrashing around inside me. It had been like that most of the day. Sometime between spelling and mathematics I started counting up the days in my head. It was almost two weeks since I'd had my eyes tested in Lunenburg. Dr. Blanchard said my new glasses should arrive by mail in about ten days. Ten days had come and gone, and there were no glasses in sight. I figured it had all been just a big cruel joke. Sometimes you've got to stop yourself from hoping too hard, and wanting too much, or you end up in your bedroom crying into your pillow over something that was never actually going to happen in the first place.

When my shoes hit the kitchen oilcloth I stopped short. Aunt Millie was sitting at the table, her arms folded, her head titled off to one side. I sensed right away that she had her nose out of joint. Could have been something big, could have been something teensy. With Aunt Millie it was always hard to tell. What had I done? Something? Nothing? Would I get chewed out for no good reason? The little bird inside me had stopped in mid-flight. One look from Aunt Millie could do that sometimes.

"Your little parcel came," she snapped, handing it over to me.

I ripped the brown package out of her hands and held it close. I wasn't used to getting mail, so that in itself was a big deal. The fact that it was my new eyeglasses made it all the sweeter. I rubbed my fingers across the place where my name and address was printed.

"Hey, you opened it!" I cried, seeing that the package had been torn open.

"Oh, for heaven's sake, Cammie Deveau, it's just eyeglasses. You act like it's something personal." She flicked her hand at me.

"You could go to jail for opening other people's mail, you know."

"And you could have told me you were getting glasses," she added indignantly.

Back in the middle of April, two ladies from Sheppard Square had pulled up in a car at the schoolhouse. They drove me away to get my eyes tested. Miss Muise set the whole thing up. She warned me not to get my hopes up too high.

"There might not be any help for you, Cammie, but I think we should at least give it a try." She paused before adding, "If you'd like your aunt to go with you, I suppose she'd be welcome." Her voice dropped off like it had been tossed over a cliff.

There was no love lost between Aunt Millie and Miss Muise. During the school year they'd had a few squabbles. Aunt Millie didn't like the idea that she wasn't the boss of me anymore.

"If that woman ever did an honest day's work I'd go through the floor," she'd sometimes say.

I've learned a thing or two about Aunt Millie over the years, enough not to take her with me when I went to see the eye doctor. I knew if I worded things just right Aunt Millie would be bound to refuse Miss Muise's offer to come along.

"Miss Muise said you should probably go with me when I get my eyes tested tomorrow. She said it would be the only decent thing for you to do," I said to Aunt Millie the day before I was set to go. I wasn't very good at making up stories. Would she believe me?

"Oh she does, does she?" Aunt Millie gave a grunt. "Well, guess what? Miss Muise doesn't get to tell *me* what to do."

She poked her thumb in her chest as she spoke. Her words came out slurred. "I'd like to know who she thinks she is. If she'd bothered to ask me, I could have told her that glasses aren't going to help your eyes. You were born like this and there's nothing anyone can do. So you just take *that* back to Miss Muise."

The other kids ran out that day to watch me leave. They all wanted to know where I was going. Miss Muise smiled and told them they were too inquisitive for their own good, and for a teeny-tiny moment I felt like someone important instead of just plain old Blind-eyed Cammie Deveau, the bootlegger's niece. I pretended I was royalty, sitting back and watching the countryside roll on by.

When I got home and told Aunt Millie all about the excursion I'd been on, and how those women even bought me fish and chips to eat, the smoke started to roll. She called Miss Muise every bad name she could think of. She even threatened to have her fired and sent back where she came from, like she had enough clout for that.

"Fish and chips," she huffed. "I wonder who paid them to do that?"

"You had your chance," I said. "Miss Muise said you should come along."

"Think I'd give her the satisfaction?" she asked.

When I had unwrapped that warm dish of fish and

chips, the most heavenly aroma filled the backseat of the car. I'd even remembered to say thank you when the lady first handed it to me. I held it on my lap and dipped my chips into a little paper cup of ketchup. I tried to make them last all the way home, but you can only eat so slowly when something is tempting you to gobble it down. I wanted to fold the brown wrapping paper up and take it home because it smelled so good, but one of the women made me hand it up to her, the empty dish and wooden fork, too.

—

I held tight to the package, protecting my glasses from Aunt Millie's clutches. She wasn't getting her paws on it again, not if I had anything to do with it.

"I should report you for this," I said sullenly.

The slap Aunt Millie delivered to my mouth made my cheeks flap, not that it hurt so bad, mostly my pride. I should have known it was coming. When would I learn? Nothing riled Aunt Millie more than when I sauced her like that, but I couldn't let her get away with it. I grabbed her hand and tried to bite it. She pulled back before I could make contact, and at the same time yanked the parcel from me.

"Give me that!" I squawked.

Her taking my glasses hurt more than the slap. She held the parcel out of my reach, waving it all around. I jumped up and tried to grab hold of it, flailing my arm in the air. No luck!

"If something comes to this house, I've got a right to open it. Whose name is on the deed?" she asked, moving the parcel all around to keep me from getting at it.

What's a deed, anyway? Just a stupid piece of paper with a name scrawled on it. I made a few more attempts at getting my glasses back.

"Why do you have to go and ruin everything, Cammie?" she asked as if she had been hurt by something. The resignation in her voice told me she was ready to give in.

"*Me* ruin things? You had no business opening my mail." I held out my hand and waited for her to give me what was mine. I knew she eventually would. She always did. Just so long as she had the upper hand for a while. That's all she usually needed. With a grunt she passed the parcel over.

My hands quivered as I fumbled with the packaging. She sat watching me like a hawk. I could feel her breath on me, silently begging me to hurry. I didn't know what her problem was, what it was about me getting something in the mail that stuck in her craw like that. She was the one who got annoyed whenever I couldn't see something. Didn't she want me to see better? Or was she just sour because Miss Muise was the one who had gotten them for me in the first place?

At first I thought they would give me just any old glasses. I could hardly believe it that day when Dr. Blanchard told me to choose the ones I liked best. Right away I wanted the gold metal frames. Dr. Blanchard made some measurements, and adjusted the frames to make them a proper fit. He promised to send them to me as soon as the lenses were put in.

I removed my eyeglasses from the package. I'd waited for that moment for so long I could hardly stand it. I made myself slow down. I knew better than to appear too anxious. If Aunt Millie saw how nervous I was she'd make a big deal about it. She'd tell everyone within earshot how I shivered and shook when I opened them up. She'd make it all into a big joke the way she always did.

"So tell me, do they think I can't spring for a lousy pair of glasses?" she asked.

So *that's* what was bothering her. Big deal! Some other time she'd be glad I was getting something free of charge.

"What's it to you?"

"Could be just a waste of their time and money," she said.

"So what? The money didn't come out of your pocket," I said as I hooked them behind my ears. Instantly, the fuzziness was gone. Everything looked clearer. Even the colours seemed brighter. It was like magic. Turning about in a circle, I tried to take it all in at once. I hurried toward the hallway mirror for a look. Aunt Millie trotted behind me.

Leaning toward the mirror, I could see the shape of my eyes and even the colour. I ran my fingers across the thin gold frames. They were perfect. I was as pleased as could be, having picked them out myself.

"Miss Muise said if they help even a little bit it would be worth it," I said.

"Oh, Miss Muise! She's just one of those do-gooders, always running around sticking their noses into everyone's business because it makes them feel important. They like to rip people's pride out from under them, that's what *they* like to do."

I hated it when Aunt Millie was on her high horse. But I didn't bother to try and defend Miss Muise. What good would it have done? Aunt Millie could justify anything she said if given half a chance.

"So, can you make out what the clock says?" she asked, all snooty-like.

The clock was all the way across the room. "I can make out the shape of it," I said, indignant-like. It was clearer than before, but I couldn't make out any of the numbers. Aunt Millie grunted.

"There you go. Just what I figured." Aunt Millie flung her hands up in the air. "I was told eyeglasses would be useless the way *your* eyes are or I'd have got them for you years ago." she said. Who would have told her that? It was the first time I'd heard it. Probably something that had just popped into her head to say that very moment.

"Do you think I didn't try everything I could have?" she continued.

Oh sure, make it sound as if you ever cared about my eyesight, I thought.

"Some people might go so far as to say Miss Muise made a fool of those do-gooders down at the Red Cross, not to mention her getting your hopes up for nothing."

I didn't care what Aunt Millie thought, having the fuzziness gone from my world sure felt worth it to me. She said a few more things, but I wasn't paying attention. I was too busy trying out my new eyeglasses, checking out how much clearer things looked. If I paid attention to everything Aunt Millie ranted on about, my head would be knotted up so tight I wouldn't be able to think.

Her voice became a soft rumble of thunder in the background. I went back to the mirror to admire myself one more time. I wasn't about to let Millie Turple ruin the moment for me. My mind soared like an eagle in the wind. My body felt light and carefree. I must have finally done something right for a change.

A sudden idea flickered in my brain as I stood leaning

in toward the mirror. I needed to see wide-open spaces. I needed to see the grass and the ground and anything else I possibly could. Racing down the hallway, I flicked the latch with my thumb and flung the front door wide open. It hit with a bang that rattled the entire house. Aunt Millie stayed close at my heels yapping like Buster, the Merry's hound from down the road, but I still wasn't listening. I ignored her the same way I ignored Buster those times he ran out to the road showing his teeth.

I dropped to my knees and touched the grass. I pulled it from the roots and ran my fingers through it. Each blade was perfectly formed, a thin green shoot growing out of the ground. I knew Aunt Millie was watching, but I didn't care. I could see things much clearer. I couldn't stop myself from being glad. The little bird was going right to town in my chest. It was dancing and flapping up a storm. I was seeing a brand new world. I looked at the tufts of dandelion flowers that were hiding in the new spring grass. I picked one to admire. Each tiny yellow petal was like a blade of sunshine. There must have been a thousand or so on its little round head. If Miss Muise had been there I would have thrown my arms around her and held tight.

"Stop rolling around on the ground, Cammie Deveau. You look like a simpleton down there," Aunt Millie said, nudging me with the toe of her shoe. "Now act like a young lady."

"Young lady!" Who did she think she was? Millie Turple, the local bootlegger, that's who, telling me to act like a young lady when there wasn't a ladylike bone in her whole body. I rolled over and looked up at her. Sunshine hit me in the face, and I put my arm across my forehead to shade it.

"You're going on twelve, Cammie Deveau. Now act like it!"

"What are you talking about? I won't be twelve until December," I said, and that was more than six months away. When it came to exaggerating, Aunt Millie was an expert. She grabbed me by the arm and pulled. My feet flopped like a rag doll's as she hauled me up.

"Leave me be. I'm testing out my new glasses," I said, smoothing my dress down in its place. I had no plans to let the whole wide world see my business.

"Just break those new glasses and see how that feels," she snorted. That kind of snapped me to attention. I wouldn't have wanted to do anything to break my new set of eyes. What could I have been thinking?

"Now come on, Cammie. Get yourself into the house. You can set the supper table." Aunt Millie made it sound as though setting the table was some grand event I wouldn't want to miss out on. I knew there wasn't much sense in arguing. We turned to go back into the house. That's when Aunt Millie let a yelp out of her.

"Hey, there!" she cried out. "There's someone standing down by the roadside gawking at us, Cammie."

I reeled around to face the road. All I could make out was a smudge of dark blue at the bottom of the driveway, even with my new set of eyes.

"Why, I think it's that Merry boy!" Aunt Millie declared, like she'd just discovered gold. "What's he hanging around here for? Looking to get another free ice cream, no doubt. Well, I'll put a stop to this. I'm not having Jim Merry's kid spying on me, the little beggar. He's nothing but trouble, that boy is."

Aunt Millie started off, stomping her way down the driveway like an elephant going after a peanut. I hurried after her. I'd already warned Evelyn not to let Aunt Millie catch him coming around. He was usually careful.

"Aunt Millie, no! He's probably just walking past. No harm done." I yanked on her arm, but she pushed me away. The blue smudge at the end of the driveway took off.

"I don't want that Merry boy coming around here, Cammie. If I catch him anywhere near this place there's going to be trouble. You got that?"

Chapter Eight

There's an easy way to get from the ground all the way to my bedroom window on the second floor. Well, maybe not so easy for me, but for Evelyn Merry it's a piece of cake. We discovered this last Saturday when Aunt Millie was getting her hair styled at the Clip 'n' Curl in Sheppard Square. Evelyn got up that tree as slick as a zoo monkey, sat on a top limb and waved down at me, sounding like a monkey would, too. I laughed so hard I thought I'd pee my pants. But then I came to my senses. I told him he'd best climb down before he fell out and broke his neck. The last thing I needed was for Aunt Millie to come home and find Evelyn Merry lying dead in the daffodils. So, even though I knew he could climb that tree, I never expected to hear tapping on my bedroom window in the middle of the night. It took me a while to realize what was going on.

"*Psst!* Cammie, *psst*…open up."

"Who is it?"

"Cammie, can you hear? It's me, Evelyn."

"Okay, okay," I whispered back, hoping he'd stop calling out my name.

I knew enough not to put the light on. The pull chain would make a loud snap if I yanked on it. I wasn't looking to have Aunt Millie come running. She could sniff out a racket in the making quicker than a hound could pick up a scent.

The moon was big and bright. It lit up my bedroom enough so that I could see to get around. My glasses. I felt around the nightstand until I found them. Hooking them behind my ears, I fixed my hair and tried to drape it about my face. I didn't want my eyeglasses to jump out at Evelyn when he saw me wearing them for the first time. It would seem like a brag, yet I could hardly wait to share the news.

I wondered what Evelyn would say when he saw them as I headed toward the window. The surprise would be obvious in his voice—he might give a whistle, he might say, "Wow!"—and I'd have to tell him to quiet down before Aunt Millie heard. I was thinking real hard on what Evelyn would say about my glasses when I finally woke up properly and realized something had to be up. Why the heck else was Evelyn Merry outside my bedroom window in the middle of the night?

I opened the window a crack. Fresh air hadn't been inside my bedroom since last summer, and the window was none too fussy about letting go. If I moved it too far it would squeak to high heaven.

"What are you doing out there?" I whispered into the crack.

"Let me in," he said.

"You've got to be kidding. It's the middle of the night... Go home."

"I can't."

"What do you mean, you can't?"

"Pa's got the shotgun out again."

I didn't know what to do. If Aunt Millie caught Evelyn in my room she'd skin us both alive. I chewed the idea over for a bit.

He got to me with a soft whisper of, "Cammie, *please*." There was a hitch in his voice, something I'd never heard before.

"Help me with the window," I whispered. Evelyn wouldn't have come here without a good reason. I knew that. Gripping the bottom of the window, I tried to push it up. Evelyn's fingers appeared beneath the sash. We eased the window up little by little. It made small squeaks as we inched it open. I held my breath. A garden snail could have moved faster, but I wasn't taking any chances.

"Not so fast," I whispered. Noises are louder late at night. I could just see Aunt Millie jumping into my room, going off the deep end the moment she saw Evelyn.

When the window was opened far enough, Evelyn stepped through. First a leg and then a shoulder emerged, and as slick as a fresh-born calf, Evelyn slid into my room.

"What's that on your face?" he asked the moment he straightened up.

"My new glasses, you dope." During the struggle to get the window open I'd forgotten all about them. I wished then I hadn't bothered to put them on.

"Here, help me get this down," I said pushing on the top of the window sash.

"I'll get it," he said, taking over. "You didn't say you were getting glasses."

So much for dumb surprises. The whole moment had been ruined.

"That's good enough," I said when the window made a few squeaks. We were too close to risk getting caught now.

Evelyn gave me the once over. I wasn't used to being examined like that. He'd see all my defects, the same ones I saw in the mirror when I got up real close.

"They look good. I bet they'll look even better in the light."

I grunted out a quick, "Thanks," annoyed that he had to see them this way. So much for my plans of showing them off for the first time. No big deal, no surprise, just like everything good that happened in my life.

Evelyn plopped himself down at the foot of my bed. The springs squawked as he swung his legs back and forth.

"Stop that!" I warned. "She'll hear."

He smelled faintly of cow manure. Little wonder, as much time as he spent in the barn with the cattle. He still had big plans of owning a sloop ox one day, something his pa kept promising and not delivering. He'd been talking about it since that first day I met him. If God were any good at all, he'd let it happen. No one should have to live a life like Evelyn Merry's without getting a break now and again.

"So, what's up?" I asked.

"Nothing's up. I just didn't want to be home is all." Evelyn sounded all tough but he didn't fool me.

"You've got a big room," he said, changing the subject real quick. He looked about from side to side, scrutinizing every corner—what he could see of it in the moonlight, that is. I could make out his hands folded on his lap. He was stalling for time. The last time his parents got into a fight he and his ma took off through the woods and ended up at Maggie Weatherbed's. They went back home in the morning once Jim Merry had sobered up. After that, everything was fine and dandy for a spell. Evelyn didn't tell me much, just little trickles here and there. I guess maybe if I had Jim Merry for a father I wouldn't want to say very much either. At least with me not knowing my father I could make him out to be whoever I wanted. I figured having a father who was a war hero sure beat the pants off having a drunk and a bully for a father, even if he wasn't man enough to go against his parents and marry my mother.

"Can't I stay here?" he asked. "Just for tonight. Till the old man straightens out. Everything'll be fine in the morning."

Kind of hard to say no to your best friend when you know he wouldn't be asking in the first place unless it was real bad.

"You can sleep on the floor, but you've got to be quiet," I said, feeling my way to the closet. The floorboards creaked.

"Cammie!" whispered Evelyn, like there was something I could do to stop the floor from squeaking. I pulled back the curtain and felt around the closet for my winter coat.

"Here, take this." I handed him a few other items of clothing and he placed them on the floor for a makeshift mattress.

"There's blankets in the trunk at the foot of my bed," I said. I heard him open the lid. He wouldn't need many. It wasn't that cold. I crawled back into bed while Evelyn made a nest on the floor. A wave of cool air touched my face as he flapped a blanket out and let it drift to the floor.

I heard him rustling the blankets, whispering, "Thanks, Cammie," before settling down for the night. I had no idea what we'd do once morning came, how we'd get Evelyn out of the house without Aunt Millie finding out.

It wasn't long before Evelyn was making sleep sounds. I wished I could shut my brain off as easily. I lay awake running things through my head. Would I spend the rest of my days in Tanner? How would I ever get away? Where would I go? Leaving Tanner would mean leaving Evelyn behind. Whose place would he go to when his old man got rowdy again?

Evelyn made a few short snorts in his sleep and I tried not to giggle. I pulled the blankets up around my neck. A thin strip of wind found its way beneath the window. A thought breezed through my brain just as I drifted off, something Evelyn had said a few months back. "You have to look out for yourself, Cammie, cause no one else is going to do it for you."

The next morning a ball of sunshine somersaulted inside my bedroom and glowed the colour of summer buttercups. I woke Evelyn at first light.

"You've got to go," I said, giving him a nudge.

The house was quiet. It wouldn't be long before Aunt Millie would be up.

"I'm hungry," Evelyn said.

"You're *hungry*?" I grunted. I wanted to get him on his way before Aunt Millie came in and caught him, and all he could say was, "I'm hungry."

"Haven't had nothing to eat since yesterday noon," he said, like I was supposed to know. "Can't you get me something for breakfast?"

"Do you think we're running a hotel?" I threw my hands up into the air the way Aunt Millie sometimes does.

He stood looking at the floor. Anyone would have thought he'd lost his best friend. I felt like apologizing. I had no business being snarky like that. Evelyn and me, we always stuck together, two misfits from Tanner—just him and me.

"I don't want to go home. Not till he's sober." He sounded pitiful.

"Wait here. I'll bring something up," I said. "But if you hear Aunt Millie, hide under the bed." He nodded, his mouth spread wide open like a pumpkin grinner.

The only thing I could find in the kitchen was a heel of bread. I plastered it with molasses and put it on a bread-and-butter plate. I poured a glass of milk. It wasn't much, but I figured it was better than an empty stomach. I remembered the tin of cookies Aunt Millie had made a few days ago and grabbed a handful. I almost dropped the food when I heard someone coming down the steps. I was frantically looking for a place to hide it when the kitchen door swung open. I jumped like a scared cat. Evelyn! Milk slopped out of the glass and ran down my hand.

"Are you nuts? If Aunt Millie…"

"Aunt Millie my foot! She's snoring and farting up a storm. If a bomb went off she wouldn't hear a thing."

He grabbed up the bread and molasses. "Thanks," he said, right before he sank his teeth in. I wished I had something better to offer him.

A swig of the milk, a quick swipe of his chin, and he was ready for more. He swallowed so loudly I thought for sure Aunt Millie would wake up. I'd never seen anyone eat so fast. I handed him the cookies. Another drink of milk and the glass was empty. He bit into a sugar cookie.

"Not bad. Your aunt can sure bake," he said.

"You sound surprised. We have to eat too, you know."

"I wasn't sure she'd have much time for baking is all." I felt strangely indignant. What did he think, Aunt Millie didn't cook and clean like everyone else?

"Would you stop taking your good old time?" My ears were pricked, listening for her to start moving about. This was taking forever.

A door slammed from upstairs. We both jumped.

"Get going!" I cried.

He grabbed the last cookie from off the sideboard and hurried for the door.

"Wait!" I whispered. Tearing the top off the cookie tin, I shoved a handful of cookies at him. He smiled, and disappeared out the backdoor.

The kitchen door opened. I turned around to face Aunt Millie. She dawdled toward the woodbox and reached down for some kindling to start a fire in the cook stove. Evelyn's blue shirt disappeared from my sight.

"Not much sense making up a fire to heat the whole outdoors," she said. I closed the door. For once I didn't mind her bossing me around.

Chapter Nine

I showed up at school wearing my glasses Monday morning, feeling like there was something special about me for the first time in my life. Miss Muise was smiling and so was I.

"How are your glasses working, Cammie?" she asked.

"Things aren't so fuzzy anymore," I said.

"Can you see what's written on the blackboard now?" Her voice was full of hope. The lines on the blackboard were still too small for me to see from that distance. I shook my head.

"How about when you're reading from a book?" she asked.

"I need to take them off when I read," I said.

Dr. Blanchard had told me I was so nearsighted I still wouldn't be able to see as well as everyone else even with the glasses, but I wasn't about to complain. Improvements don't have to be gigantic to count. I hesitated over saying anything more to Miss Muise. I didn't expect her to understand. She doesn't know how my eyes work, what I see and what I don't. Sometimes it doesn't make sense to me.

"I never stop hoping for miracles," Miss Muise said. She sounded disappointed.

"Seeing the little pebbles on the ground is a miracle," I said.

"Oh, Cammie! I wish you could see what's on the blackboard is all, but I suppose any improvement is worthwhile." I was glad to hear her say that. "If I was running the world you'd see as good as everyone else."

Miss Muise sighed. I could tell there was more she wanted to say.

"There's a school, Cammie." She began slowly, carefully choosing her words. "They teach blind and visually impaired children. I've known about it for a while now, but, well, you know what your aunt's like." She let out another small sigh. "I didn't think she'd approve, and yet it's not fair to keep this to myself. I've been wrestling with the whole thing. Do I tell you or don't I? First, wondering if it is fair to let you know about something that you might never be able to have, then deciding that keeping secrets isn't fair either. But I told myself some things are out of my hands. I like to think that all things are possible, even if they're not probable."

Miss Muise went on to tell me all about that special school in the city. She had my attention the moment she mentioned Halifax. I listened to everything she had to say. Her words bubbled like soda and vinegar as she spoke. The excitement in her voice made that little bird inside me start to dance.

"There's swimming and parties and walks in the Public Gardens. And oh, Cammie." Miss Muise had gasped like she was picturing it all in her head just for me. "You'd get to have a decent education and learn all sorts of skills, things you won't get in public school." It sounded so great I was scared to get my hopes up. She took my hand. Her skin was soft and warm.

This could be my ticket out of Tanner, the one I've been waiting for, I thought. Not to mention, I knew a certain someone who was living in the city thanks to an envelope Aunt Millie had left lying around when I was small. Aunt Millie didn't have an inkling I knew where my mother was. I'd kept that information to myself. She always made it sound as though my mother lived a million miles from here. She might as well, considering she never came to visit.

"The best thing that could happen would be getting yourself as far away from your aunt as you can," Miss Muise continued. There was an awkward pause. "You do know what I mean, don't you, Cammie?"

My throat made a strange squawk. There were things I wanted to tell Miss Muise, things that no one else knew, but I didn't know where to start. She might be able to get me glasses, but there was nothing she could do about the rest of it. How could I tell her about the goings on in our house? And how could I tell her about all the rackets that had taken place there over the years? And above all that, how could I tell her that my very own mother never came to visit? How would someone like Miss Muise, with her soda and vinegar bubbles, understand any of that? I tried to speak while Miss Muise stood there holding onto my hand.

"I really want to go, Miss Muise," I said finally.

Miss Muise was quiet for a spell. I thought maybe I'd said something wrong.

"Cammie, your aunt would have to give her consent for that to happen," she said. "Do you think she would do that?"

I was certain Aunt Millie would kick up a stink the moment I mentioned this special school, especially if she found out Miss Muise had anything to do with it.

"Can't I just tell them I want to go?" I asked. Why did I need Aunt Millie's say-so? I could speak for myself.

"You'll need the consent of your next of kin," she said. "Those are the rules."

"My next of kin?"

"I'm afraid so. I could talk to your aunt if you think it would make a difference."

Despite her offer to speak with Aunt Millie, Miss Muise thought it was a lost cause. I could hear it in her voice. I didn't much blame her. Aunt Millie was about as cooperative as a cat being given a bath. We'd both seen plenty of evidence of that during the school year. Still, lost cause or not, there had to be some way for me to get to that school.

My smile felt as though it would never end. I knew I should thank Miss Muise for telling me all about this new school in the city, but I couldn't get the words unjumbled in my head. Then I started to feel like an idiot, standing there at her desk with a stupid grin on my face. I had so many things in place that I had planned to say. I'd spent time the day before practising in my room. I wanted to thank her for helping me get my glasses and for having Evelyn do my copying for me. And I wanted to say I appreciated when she made the kids stop calling me Blind-eyed Cammie, even though they still said it when she was nowhere handy to hear. I wanted to thank her for all the crayons she'd lent me and for taking my pictures home with her because I didn't want Aunt Millie to see them ever again. I had practised what I would say until the words flowed smooth as cream from my lips. But as I stood there at Miss Muise's desk, my mind screamed out that it was stupid, pathetic, and hopeless to be gushing with the gratitude I was feeling. And then I heard Aunt Millie's voice in my head.

Miss Muise is just trying to make her job easier, that's all. And that extra splash of vinegar soon made the bubbles fizzle away to nothing.

—

When I got home from school, Aunt Millie was lying down with one arm across her eyes, the other hanging limply over the edge of the chesterfield. She moaned when she heard me walk across the living room floor and told me to keep it down.

"I'm not feeling so good. Might be the flu," she said, like she thought that would fool me. It might have worked when I was a kid, but it didn't fool me anymore. Disgust hit me hard. She'd promised a while back this wouldn't happen again.

"You're loaded," I said.

"Oh, Cammie Deveau, you're exaggerating again. Pick up around will you, and start something for supper?" she groaned. I stood looking down at her. She opened one eye. "Don't just stand there. Get moving." She made for me to move on my way.

"What are you going to do when I'm not here?" I said.

"Oh, Cammie, where else are you going to be?" Aunt Millie asked as I stormed out of the room.

I spent the evening in my bedroom reading through the *Standard* magazines. I looked at all the places the king and queen visited when they finally made it to Halifax. I read about their trip to city hall, and the reception that was held on Citadel Hill. I looked at the photographs of them making up to some triplets in a baby carriage, and the queen scrutinizing some veterans. I read all the words and looked at the pictures, and when I got to the end I looked at them again. I didn't bother coming out until morning.

I had no idea how I was going to tell Aunt Millie about that school in Halifax.

Miss Muise said she could get me enrolled for the coming fall if only Aunt Millie would agree. Fat chance of that happening. It was stupid for me to even think of asking her. Already it was May, nearly the end of the school year. How in the world was I going to bring it up to Aunt Millie? Miss Muise had offered to talk to her, but I knew that would be a mistake. It would set Aunt Millie into a tailspin. She'd dig her heels in and say no just to spite Miss Muise.

That night I tried to dream up that school in my head, but I didn't know where to start. I'd never heard of a dormitory or dining hall or even a music room before, let

alone tried to picture them in my mind. For the first time
in my life, I was stuck. I couldn't imagine what a brand
new life at that school would be like. I knew the only way I
was going to picture it right was if I got to see it for myself.
I had to plan just what I was going to do, how I was going
to go about getting this new life of mine in gear.

Just then a thought popped into my head. I sat up in bed.
Aunt Millie wasn't my only next of kin. What about my
grandmother? Why couldn't she give permission? It might
be a long shot, but it was worth a try. She didn't know me,
but all that could change under the right circumstances.
My mind starting going a hundred miles an hour. Surely
there was some way to convince my grandmother to help.
All things are possible. Miss Muise even said. I wasn't
about to call it quits. Besides, I figured I'd probably stand
a better chance with my grandmother than Aunt Millie.

I reached under my mattress and pulled out the envelope I'd been saving since I was small. The writing was
faded and the paper was yellow. I held it up and looked at it
for the hundredth time since I'd learned how to read. The
return address said *Burnham Street, Halifax, Nova Scotia*,
and no matter how many times I looked at the faded writing, it wasn't going to change.

"I got a letter from your mother today," Aunt Millie had
said the day it arrived.

"Where is she?" I asked, ready to jump out of my britches.

"You know what? She didn't even say. She could be anywhere by now," said Aunt Millie. "Off seeing the world, I guess."

"Read it to me. Read it," I begged, thinking surely there was something Aunt Millie had missed.

"It's up in the clouds by now," she said, pointing to the woodstove.

"You burned it?" I howled.

"Oh for heaven's sake, Cammie Deveau, you can't even read," she said. I begged and pleaded until she finally told me what my mother had written.

"Not much, really," she said, giving in. "Just that the weather was fine and she hoped we were doing good. She bought a pink dress the other day for some party she was going to."

"Did she ask about me?" I was nearly beside myself with want.

"She's your mother. Of course she asked about you," said Aunt Millie.

I was brimming with joy that day. My mother had finally written! She was really out there making her mark, just the way Aunt Millie had promised.

I spied something white lying on the table. "Is this the envelope?" I asked. I looked at the writing but it made no sense to me. I held it to my chest, hoping I'd be able to feel her every word in my heart. It was the only thing I had that belonged to my mother, and I'd held on to it since that day.

I slipped the envelope back into its hiding place. Halifax was probably the last place Aunt Millie would want me to go. If I had thrown the envelope in the stove the way Aunt Millie told me to that day I wouldn't have a clue as to where my mother was. At least I had a place to start. My mind was made up. Not only was I going to get to Halifax, I was going to find my mother in the bargain. I'd put the questions to her, find out where she's been all this time. Aunt Millie could go jump in the lake for all I cared. I was going to get to that blind school in Halifax and learn how to make my way in the world. I'd get my grandmother to sign the papers for me. I didn't know how, and I didn't know when. But one thing I knew for sure, I was going to do something to change my life.

Chapter Ten

*Come in, come in, come in, my dear, my grandmother says,
her voice sweet like cherry pie at the thought of finding her
long-lost granddaughter. She's as pleased as punch to find
out we're related when I tell her, and me, I can't seem to stop
smiling. If there's such a place as on top of the world, I think
I've found it. I'm not even shy about the thought of getting
to know her. The moment I ask her if I can go to the Halifax
School for the Blind, she says she'd be a fool not to let me go.
Then there's Aunt Millie, standing there like she's queen for
the day, hands resting on her hips as she says, "Over my dead
body, Cammie Deveau."*

Evelyn ran into Mae Cushion's store to ask for directions
to my grandmother's house. I once asked Aunt Millie if
we could swing past her place to have a look, but she said
she wouldn't waste the effort. I couldn't take a chance that

Aunt Millie was exactly where she was supposed to be, sitting at the Clip 'n' Curl having her hair set, so I hid behind the lilac bush right next to Mae's piazza. I could usually get out of going into Sheppard Square on Saturday by telling Aunt Millie I had oceans of homework or else had some reading I wanted to do. She knew how long it took me to read and write so she usually didn't question it. Eventually, she stopped asking if I was going. Saturday became a day of freedom, the day when Evelyn and I could do as we pleased without worrying that we'd get caught.

"It's the biggest house in Sheppard Square. Head on down Maple Street. You can't miss it," Mae had said. When Evelyn came out and told me that, I have to admit I felt a tiny bit special, even though her having this grand old house never did me a lick of good growing up.

"Whatever you want from Mrs. Deveau, it must be important for you to come all this way," Mae had said. She likely thought she was going to weasel the information out of him, but it didn't work. Mae might ask nosy questions, but Evelyn knew when and how to keep his mouth shut. I could always count on him for that.

"We've got smooth sailing," said Evelyn as we turned down Maple Street. "We don't even have to pass the hairdresser's." It felt good to know that things were going in my favour. Smooth sailing sounded pretty decent to me.

Tarpapered buildings make a good hiding place. I found that out after the first few moments spent crouching behind my grandmother's woodshed that day. I started to think I could get used to spying on people, not that I could do any of it without Evelyn by my side. I figured we made a pretty good team, even if I was the one doing the say-so. Maybe Evelyn would have a different story to tell.

With a good view of the house and front yard, I waited for Evelyn to describe it all to me. No worries about getting caught by the old gal so long as we were careful. Smiling, I listened to what he had to say about the house and verandah, the shiny new Roadster sitting in the pebbled driveway, all the little details he knew I'd want to hear.

"There's a porch swing out on the verandah, too. It's dark green but needs a new coat of paint to spruce it up." Excitement was tumbling inside me so fast that I wasn't sure I could get it stopped.

"I always wanted a porch swing," I said. I knew Evelyn would take notice of the dreamy sound in my voice, but I didn't care.

"What's wrong with *our* swing?" he asked, miffed by the sounds of it. Our swing was just an old tire that Evelyn rigged up to a hardwood tree not far from our secret camp.

"Is there a pointed roof? How about an attic window? What about a flower garden? I think I see some pink out front. Is that flowers?" Questions were streaming out of me as fast as they entered my brain. This was my grandmother's house, the place where my daddy had grown up and played, and the place where my mother and grandparents pulled off the battle of the century. This was home, the place I belonged.

A raven cried and the tree branches let out a tight squeak in the breeze. I couldn't stand it any longer. Watching and waiting wasn't doing a thing. I was itching to have her say I could go to Halifax. I marched toward my grandmother's big white house, drawn to it like a fly to honey. I was through dreaming up this meeting in my head. I was ready to take action.

Evelyn pulled on my arm.

"This isn't the plan," he said as I marched toward the house. Our plan was that he'd sneak me out here to Sheppard Square to see if we could catch sight of my grandmother, maybe see what she looked like, and then go down to Mae Cushion's store for some jawbreakers to celebrate. We were only planning to check the place out this time. No part of our plan had me knocking at her door and facing her right then and there. We were still working on a way to get her to sign the paper for me. I didn't expect the old battleaxe to be all sweet and nice, like when I dreamt her up in my mind, but I aimed to find out for sure.

Sometimes you've got to act on the thought that's in your brain the very moment it gets there. If you let it rumble around a little it loosens its grip and pretty soon the idea slips away. I knew if I waited I'd probably change my mind. My new life was awaiting me. I had to get to Halifax. I had serious business to conduct.

It took only three good knocks before the old biddy answered the door. The little bird in my chest was beating its wings frantically, telling me to run.

Sorry little bird, but I just can't do that.

"What is it you want?" The breeze caught her question and blew it back in my face. I detected an air of annoyance. My knees wobbled as I waited to see what her reaction would be once I told her who I was.

"You're my grandmother," I stated, tough and mean, because I figured the old girl should squirm a little, and I wasn't really sure how to lead up to stating my purpose. All those years of her ignoring my very existence had built up inside me. There was plenty more where that came from, and plenty more that needed ironing out if I was going to get her to cooperate with me. I had to hold back.

"What nonsense are you going on about, child?"

What did she mean by nonsense? I could tell this wasn't going to be a piece of cake, but I had known that long before I rapped at the door.

"It's not nonsense. You are *so* my grandmother. Aunt Millie told me the whole story." There. She'd know right off that she couldn't discourage me, not the way she'd discouraged my parents. Thanks to Aunt Millie I knew all her tricks. I was ready for anything she had to dish out.

"Cammmieee." Evelyn squeezed the word out, low like I was the only one who was supposed to hear. Fine time for him to get squeamish on me. It was too late to back out. I had to get to the bottom of it all, see what she had to say for herself, why she had ignored me all my life, without making her annoyed at me in the bargain. Above all, I needed her cooperation.

Evelyn pulled on my arm again, but I had my feet firmly planted. I wasn't stepping foot off the verandah until I got what I wanted.

"And what proof do you have of this?" She made a small snort that left my face feeling hot.

"Because I…because…" The words were getting tangled on my tongue.

"If I'm, as you say, your grandmother, you need to offer me some proof of this. I can hardly believe some young girl I've never seen before, can I?"

Good. I figured she knew I was onto her.

Clearing her throat, my grandmother asked us to come inside. This was getting more complicated by the minute.

"I'll make tea," she said as we followed her through the house. I looked over at Evelyn and shrugged my shoulders. I never thought she was going to make me prove who I was.

—

My grandmother looked at us across the top of her teacup and silently sipped her tea. The springs on the chesterfield squeaked as Evelyn wiggled uncomfortably.

Two fancy cups of tea were sitting on a little table in front us. I added a bit of cream and stirred them with a spoon. I wondered how long it would be before my grandmother would start walking the questions to me. I hoped Evelyn would be a little help.

"Drink up," she said with a tiny nod. "A good hostess never drinks alone." It seemed like some devious act of trickery on her part. She would try and trip me up, tell me I was just packing a bunch of lies. I took a quick sip of tea and set my teacup down. Evelyn did the same. I told myself I was prepared for anything she could throw my way.

"So tell me, is there a reason why you think I'm your grandmother or did you just dream it up one day?" she finally asked.

"My aunt Millie told me so." No way was she going to make me back down now.

"And who is this Aunt Millie of yours? Is she someone I should know?" She set her teacup down.

"Know her? Of course you know her. You were best friends when you were young! Well, maybe you weren't so young, but Aunt Millie was." No sense beating around the bush. I figured it was best to tell it the way it was.

"My best friend, you say?" There was fake disbelief in her voice. She pretended not to know.

"Only you stopped being fun. You got all serious about your money and that ended you two being friends. Who knows, maybe you were scared your husband would start chasing after her. Men do that, you know."

"Do what?"

"Chase after Aunt Millie. The men flock to her like crows to a gut pile."

"You don't say! And you think my Herman might have been tempted?"

I gave a beats-me kind of shrug. "No telling with Aunt Millie. She's not bad looking, you know."

My grandmother took a stingy sip of tea. "Just how old are you, my dear?"

"I'm eleven." Her question kind of threw me. What difference did it make how old I was?

"I'd have to say you're far too young to be a granddaughter of mine."

"I just know what Aunt Millie told me." Doubt stuck its

tongue out at me. Aunt Millie better not have lied about any of this.

"What *did* your aunt tell you? I'd be interested in hearing.You still haven't explained how any of this makes you my granddaughter."

I had to go slow. Old people don't always catch on to things if you don't. This was my only chance to make her understand.

"Your son, Charles, got my mother in the family way."

"My son Charles, you say? Oh dear!" She took another sip of tea.

"But you already know this." She was trying to distract me.

"I do?"

This was no time for her to be playing dumb.

"Of course you do."

Who was she trying to kid? Why was she pretending that she couldn't remember? It hadn't happened *that* long ago.

"There was that big fight you all had because you wouldn't let your son marry my mother. Then your son, my father, went off and got himself killed in the war. So you probably figured it didn't matter about me. It probably feels like you don't even have a grandchild."

"I see." Her words were slow and cold. I had to do something quick before she just sent me on my way.

"But I don't blame you. I might have done the same, and it wouldn't have been a problem for me if my mother had stuck around. It's really all her fault." There. I hoped that would help smooth things out.

There was a long pause as I waited for her to down the last of her tea and say something.

"Well, my dear, I thank you for this entertaining story, but I'm afraid that's all it is—a story, a bunch of gibberish." Her teacup clinked when she set it down on the saucer.

"It's not gibberish. It's the truth. I promise! Aunt Millie told me!"

How was I going to make her understand? All I wanted was for her to sign the paper for me. Then I'd be out of her hair. My brand new life depended upon it.

My lips began to tremble. If I started bawling, I'd never forgive myself.

"Let's say it's the truth, that this whole fairy tale holds some credence." She was waving her hand elegantly in the air as she spoke. The sunlight coming through the window struck the rings on her hand and they sparkled. "What in the name of good sense does any of this have to do with me now? If you're looking for money, young lady, I'm afraid you've come to the wrong place. I venture to say you had no interest in me before now."

"I don't want your money." What was she talking about?

"All I want is for you to sign a paper so that I can go to blind school. See, my eyes are small. I can't see too good. But Miss Muise told me all about this school in Halifax and I really want to go. Not just to get away from Aunt Millie, but to learn how to do things so that I can get a good job when I grow up. I don't want to end up looking after Aunt Millie when she gets old. You can't really blame me for that. Only she won't let me go. She didn't want me to go to regular school, so why would she let me go off to Halifax? The last place she probably wants me to go is Halifax. But don't you see? You could sign."

"Me? Sign a paper? I'm afraid you've confused me." She held her hand to her forehead. I knew that wasn't a good sign.

"I can't go to that school unless my next of kin gives their consent. Aunt Millie won't let me go, but she's not my only next of kin—you're my kin too. That's all I want, to get out of Tanner and go to Halifax."

This was becoming more complicated by the minute.

"All Cammie wants is for you to give your permission, Mrs. Deveau. She doesn't want anything else from you. Just your name on a paper." I looked over at Evelyn, glad that he jumped in to help. I was running out of things to say. The situation was looking none too promising. My grandmother was a stubborn woman. Then again, I knew a thing or two about stubbornness myself.

She paused for a time. I figured she was considering my proposal. I made one final plea.

"I won't tell a soul you're my grandmother. I promise." I figured that would do it. I motioned as though I were buttoning my lip. I hoped I was convincing.

"Let me get my sweater," said Mrs. Deveau after a brief silence. "I need to show you something, my dear."

———

We followed my grandmother down the road. I wanted to ask her where the heck we were going. When we turned off Maple Street, I was even more confused.

"Where is she taking us?" I whispered to Evelyn.

"A cemetery, I think," he said in disbelief.

I jabbed him in the ribs. "Quiet," I warned. He'd spoken quite loudly. What if my grandmother heard him?

We neared a large tree and stopped. My grandmother stood in front of a tombstone with her head bowed. I thought she might be saying a prayer. I'd never seen anyone pray before except in school, when we all recited the Lord's Prayer, but this was for real.

"This must be where your father is buried," whispered Evelyn.

Finally she moved to the left so that the tombstone was clearly visible.

"What does it say, Evelyn?"

I moved closer to the stone. Would it say something I wouldn't want to know? My father was dead. What else was there?

"It says, *Herman Raymond Deveau, Beloved husband and father. 1869–1938*," said Evelyn.

"I know my grandfather's dead," I said indignantly. "He died before I was born."

"There's more, Cammie," Evelyn said. "*Charles Herman Deveau sadly missed 1903–1925.*"

I moved toward the stone and got down on my knees. I traced my finger inside the carved letters, feeling the date again and again.

"So you see, my dear, my Charles couldn't possibly be your father. He died long before you were ever born. I'm afraid this Aunt Millie of yours has been feeding you lies," said Mrs. Deveau.

—

The king and queen must be the happiest people in the world. I've looked through the pictures in those old *Standard* magazines a million times over the years. I don't think a day goes by when someone doesn't give that woman flowers, leastways not while she was in Canada that time around.

Here you go, Your Majesty. I used to pretend I was one of those lucky girls wearing a ruffled dress and a crinoline, bowing before the queen and passing her a big bouquet of posies. I would practise my curtsy for hours in my bedroom. Then I'd repeat my grandmother's name, practise it like she was royalty—Sophia Deveau, Queen of Sheppard Square—which made me a princess. Knowing I had her for a grandmother had at least made me feel like I was something more than the bootlegger's niece all these years.

Chapter Eleven

We walked to Mae Cushion's general store for some candy before heading back to Tanner. There wasn't a scrap of wind to be had, and the air felt heavy with defeat. *Now what?* I wanted to ask, but couldn't bring myself to say anything without blubbering like a baby. I didn't feel like talking to anyone. What was there to say? At least Evelyn wasn't trying to make me feel better by saying a bunch of dumb things. We walked along, carrying the silence between us. I could usually count on him for that.

Once we paid for our candy we sat out on Mae Cushion's piazza for a few minutes, but then Evelyn said we'd better get going in case Aunt Millie came along.

"I know, let's go to the river," he said.

I didn't feel much like going, but it sure beat going home to an empty house and waiting for Aunt Millie. The air was cool, but the sun felt warm on my face. I kept rolling the day around in my head, dissolving it like the jawbreaker I had in my mouth, trying to make it small enough for me to swallow.

By the time we turned down the Lake Ridge Road, the ache in my throat had all but melted away like butter on a hot pancake—nearly gone, yet not quite.

"Why would she lie like that?" I asked when I was finally ready to speak.

"I guess she doesn't want you to know who your pa is," Evelyn said, shrugging his shoulders.

"But why the big lie? It doesn't make any sense. Now I don't know who my father is, and if I ask her she'll come up with another lie."

Maybe I'd never get the life I wanted.

"Are you going to tell her what you know?" asked Evelyn.

That's what Aunt Millie needed—for someone to slap the truth in her face.

I didn't answer. I knew if I did I'd just start bawling.

On our way to the river Evelyn started talking. He told me all the things I needed to hear, even those things he probably didn't believe himself. He said I was better off not having a grandmother, that sooner or later Aunt Millie would come around, and I'd get to go to that blind school in the city. He talked the most he had talked in a long time.

"There's no sense crying over spilled milk," he finally said.

But I don't even know who I am anymore, I wanted to bleat. Good thing I don't always say what I want. I'd have probably strung off more curse words than Aunt Millie, maybe even invented a few of my own in the process. We stood on the riverbank looking down into the water, listening to the birds, feeling the cool air.

"Let's go for a swim. The water looks warm," said Evelyn. He pulled off his socks and dangled his feet into the river, tempting me to give in.

"It's kind of early for swimming," I said.

"Scared to get a little chill?" Evelyn teased as he emptied his pockets.

"Who's scared?" I asked.

I kicked the shoes from my feet one at a time. They flew up high in the air, nearly hitting Evelyn in the head. I laughed and pulled my socks off. Evelyn was right, whining and crying wouldn't change anything.

Barefoot, I ran toward the edge of the river, stopping short when I realized I still had my glasses on. I folded them up and set them on a flat rock, safe where they wouldn't get broken. No way did I want anything to happen to my glasses, not after the rigmarole I went through to get them.

I got a run on and jumped in, screaming, "Geronimo!" at the top of my lungs. A thousand invisible knife blades pierced my skin as I plunged feet first into the water. I wanted to swim for shore, but was too cold to even try. I let out a series of screams and yelps.

Evelyn stood on the riverbank watching. "Hang to her, Cammie!" he laughed.

Once the initial shock was over, I got used to the cold water and stopped screaming like a banshee. My dress bunched up around my waist. I pushed the bundlesome mass beneath the water. Air bubbles spitted and sputtered as the fabric became wet. I'd never swum with a dress on before. The weight of the wet fabric tugged at me. We should have planned ahead, maybe brought our swim clothes along, but real life has a way of making you do things you haven't planned.

"Gonna let some girl get the best of you?" I hollered out at Evelyn.

Seconds later water hit my face, and the river was carrying Evelyn's yelps downstream. He slapped the icy water, making his way over to where I was.

"That water *does* have a bite to it," he said.

"Did you think I was just being a baby?" My arms and legs were starting to warm up. I moved about, kicking my legs, stretching my arms. Before I knew it we were having a game of water tag, laughing and squealing, enjoying the moment. I pushed aside the events of the day. We'd just have to come up with another plan. I wasn't stumped yet.

I saw the opposite bank and dog-paddled toward it. It wasn't that far and the water was shallow. Evelyn was right. You don't need good eyesight to swim.

"Come back here, Cammie! You're too far from shore," cried Evelyn right out of the blue. Too far? What he was talking about? Wasn't this the narrow place where I'd practised last fall?

I turned around so quickly that I didn't know which way it was to shore. I thought I knew, but then I didn't. What if I was out over my head? What if I couldn't touch bottom? The extra weight from my clothing pulled on me. A sharp pain hit me in my right side. I couldn't see Evelyn's head sticking up in the water. I cried out to him. He'd know what to do. A mouthful of water made me cough.

"Are you okay, Cammie?"

I tried to answer. Nothing came out but a gush of air. The pain in my side burned like a hot iron. Frantically, I started to stroke my way toward the sound of Evelyn's voice.

"You're going the wrong way, Cammie!" cried Evelyn.

"Where are you?" I managed to gasp out.

"Over here." Water blurred my eyes. I couldn't see a thing.

My arms and legs ached like crazy. My wet dress dragged me down farther. I could feel myself sinking. I reached my hand up, feeling the air, hoping Evelyn was there. When I couldn't find him I yelled and then I yelled some more.

"Calm down, Cammie! Take it easy, Cammie! Just take it easy!" Evelyn's voice was shaky.

"I'm drowning!" I coughed and sputtered between screams. Evelyn's voice was mingled somewhere amongst my shouts for help, but I couldn't make sense out of what he was saying. I was going to die. It was a fact. I hadn't even had time to get my new life in gear.

There was a large splash not far from me. Sinking beneath the water, I pulled myself up for a quick breath of air. Numb all over, I struggled to keep my head above water. I thought I could hear another voice, but at that point I didn't care. All I could think about was making it out of the water. In the midst of the chaos I found something to grab fast to. Evelyn! It had to be. The fabric of his shirt was beneath my fingertips.

"You're okay, Cammie," Evelyn said. "You're okay. Hold fast. Just hold fast."

We were moving, and it was all I cared about.

"Kick your legs!" he said, and I did. I would have done anything Evelyn said.

My legs and arms were trembling. I squeezed my eyes tight. When I opened them I'd be safe. That's all I concentrated on.

When we reached the riverbank, I clawed and scrambled my way out of the water. The breeze chilled me to the bone. Teeth chattering, I felt along the ground, crawling on all fours. All I wanted was to find my glasses and go home.

"Come on, Cammie. I'll take you home," said Evelyn. There was a queer sound in his voice just then like he'd hit a snag. I knew something wasn't right. He was mad at me for nearly drowning. I could tell. I found my glasses and put them on, turned toward him to see what was up. Someone else was climbing out of the water, someone tall and thin.

"You leave that little blind girl alone," came a voice hot with anger. He looked to be shaking his fist in the air. I gasped and brought my hands up to my mouth. I knew that voice. I'd heard it before outside Aunt Millie's kitchen door.

"What's wrong with your head, boy, jumping into the river this time of the year? You could have drowned that little girl. Good thing I was coming down the road and heard her crying else she'd have drowned for sure."

Jim Merry's long arms reached out at Evelyn. The sound of a hand hitting flesh made me flinch. Evelyn let out a cry.

"There's plenty more where that came from," said Jim Merry, sounding about as hateful as a grizzly bear.

I didn't wait to gather up my socks and shoes. I hurried down the path toward the main road. I didn't turn around. Sticks along the path pinched the soles of my feet, but I didn't stop. Moments later, Evelyn caught up to me. He took hold of my arm and led me home. He didn't say a word as we walked along, but I heard him make a sniffle or two. I knew if I said anything to him I'd just start blubbering. On a day when you find out your life is nothing but a lie, only to have that life be saved by a man of the lowest degree, there really isn't much to do but blubber.

—

My clothes were heaped into a wet ball on my bedroom floor. Changed and dry, I was warming up. The *Standard* magazines were lying on the foot of my bed, all the photos of the king and queen's trip to Canada the year I was born. I ripped the smiles from their faces and threw the pieces on the floor. What right did they have to be off gallivanting around the countryside months before the war broke out? I hated them. I hated their happiness and their beautiful clothes. I hated the people who stood for hours waiting to catch a glimpse of them when they drove by. Didn't they have anything better to do with their time? There were people in the world who were starving, people with no homes and no fancy clothes, people without fathers or mothers to care about them, people who didn't ask to be born with flaws, but who got them just the same. Who did they think they were? I marched downstairs to find Aunt Millie. There were things I had to say.

"You lied!" I screamed. She was setting out some bottles for the evening ahead.

"Lied about what?" she asked. "And why's your hair wet?"

"Everything! My whole life, that's what! Everything you told me was a lie! I'm not Cammie Deveau, I'm Cammie Nobody!" I fought hard to hold back my tears. My bottom lip wouldn't stay in place.

"Oh, Cammie, you're being overly dramatic again. I don't know what you want from me."

"I want to know who my father is and why you lied. Is it Jim Merry?" I asked, making a wild stab in the dark. I was afraid of the answer, but I needed to know. Maybe that was the real reason she never wanted me to have anything to do with Evelyn. Maybe it had nothing to do with his father being a bully.

"Jim Merry," she snorted. "Now that's just ridiculous. If Jim Merry was your father I'd have left you on the doorstep down at the orphan house myself. Why can't you just leave good enough alone, Cammie?"

"Because I don't know who I am!"

"You're my niece. That should be enough for you. Some

kids don't have anyone. You should be glad you have someone." She turned and went back to what she was doing.

"Why won't you tell me?" I cried out in frustration.
Tears were flowing at a steady stream; my chest was making quick jumps each time I sniffled. Aunt Millie stopped
what she was doing and let out a big sigh.

"I made a promise to Brenda, okay? I might be a lot of
things, Cammie, but I keep my word. Besides, you knowing who your father is won't change anything. He didn't
want the responsibility back then and he doesn't want it
now. Some men aren't born to be fathers. So just drop it,
okay? Some things we're best off not knowing."

Her words hit me in the core, snapping that little bird's
wing in two like it was nothing. All these years thinking
that my father was dead were a whole lot better than
knowing he didn't want me either. I was disposable, a one-
time baby to hold and then let go of. Why couldn't I have
decent parents like most everyone else?

All I wanted was someone to care about me, to get me
away from Tanner and Aunt Millie's bunch. Was that too
much to ask for? Maybe I should have drowned in the
river. Would it even matter if I had? Would life in Tanner
be any different without me in it? To top it off, Jim Merry
ended up being the one to save me. Some knight in shining
armour I've got—one of the most despicable human

beings I know. Figures, in a way—that's all the knight I deserve.

"I almost drowned today, as if you'd care." I held in my fear as I spoke the words. I didn't want her to see. Every inch of my body trembled, but I forced myself not to give in. I don't even know why I bothered to tell her, why I needed to know what her reaction would be.

She didn't let on she'd heard.

"Did you hear me? I almost drowned in the river," I whispered. She looked at me, not saying a word. What was I was expecting, for her to run to my side, for her to gush over me and tell me how glad she was that I was all right? Fat chance of that ever happening.

"I heard," she said flatly. She picked up a bottle of moonshine and set it on the sideboard. "What the devil were you doing down there?"

Chapter Twelve

"It's been reported to me that you've been seen hanging around town with that Merry boy. Didn't you promise to stay away from him? I told you he was trouble," said Aunt Millie. Should have known that bit of gossip would reach her ears before the weekend was over.

"I guess you're not the only one with secrets," I said, snarky as anyone who'd been lied to their entire life would be. Since I'd found out who my father wasn't, I'd been trying to get Aunt Millie to spill the beans about who he was. She was a hard nut to crack.

"Don't get smart with me, young lady," she said, leaning her head over the kitchen sink. It was Aunt Millie's weekly peroxide routine, just a few touches to keep it highlighted. She was always careful not to overdo. A few years back she'd got a little carried away and her hair ended up dry as rope. That didn't discourage her, though. Not like it might some people. Once the frizz started to grow out a little, she was back bleaching it again. But after that I was in charge of the peroxide while she looked after rubbing it in.

"Let's get this over with before someone shows up," she said, swatting the air as she reached for the towel on the back of the chair. I was all for getting it over with. Sometimes on Sunday afternoon I'd head off to our secret camp. Spending hours in my bedroom had its advantages. Aunt Millie never bothered to think I'd be anywhere else, so long as I was at the table come mealtime. Most times, Evelyn would be waiting for me at the camp when I got there. Today, I was going to try extra hard to show up. We hadn't had a chance to talk about what had happened yesterday, and I kind of figured we should.

The peroxide bottle was next to the sink. I picked it up and unscrewed the top. Aunt Millie thinks she looks just like that movie star, Betty Grable. People agreeing with her sets her right in her glory.

"Do you think these babies are worth a million bucks?" she squealed one time, hauling her hem up over her knee. That was right after Aunt Millie had heard that Betty Grable's legs had been insured for a million dollars. Someone in the kitchen that night let out a whistle. All evening long, Aunt Millie strutted around like she thought she was something else.

"Are you going to tell me who my father is?" I asked, holding the bottle over her hair. I had the advantage, what with her wanting something from me now. If I didn't per-oxide her hair, who would? She'd rather eat pig liver than have *that* secret come out.

"Are you still on that same kick?" she asked.

This wasn't a kick, some whim that I'd forget about over-night. This was my life. Why the big secret? Everyone has a father. Why didn't she just tell me and be done with it?

"Hurry up now, Cammie, I haven't got all day," she said, impatient like she always was whenever I asked her ques-tion she didn't want to answer.

I poured a few drops over her hair and she worked it through. She's fussy how she wants it done.

"Well…" I niggled.

"Well what?"

"Is he someone from Tanner?"

I added a bit more peroxide.

"Stop asking so many questions and do my hair. If I think you need to know something, I'll tell you."

I continued to pour.

"That's enough now," she said, but I didn't stop. I kept on pouring as spite worked its magic all the way to my fingers. For a few short moments I was in heaven.

"That's enough now, Cammie. I said that's enough!"

She stomped her foot.

"Don't tell me what to do!" I screamed as I dumped the rest of the peroxide over her head. Aunt Millie started to wail. I threw the empty bottle with a fist full of nastiness. It caught her in the leg. She let out an even louder yelp, turning around as she held her wet hair up off her forehead.

"Rinse this out of my hair right now," she said stomping her foot again. She was still yelling and stomping when I ran out the door.

One final "Get back here, Cammie" reached my ears. Did she really think I was going to listen to her anytime soon? Mess around with my life and see what happens.

—

"I hope Pa ends up dead in some ditch," Evelyn said, kicking at a small root inside our secret camp later that day. He was still hurting from yesterday. I could hear it in his voice.

"You don't mean that, Evelyn," I said. What else could I say? What had happened at the river was proof enough for me that he had every right to feel that way, but wishing Jim Merry dead wouldn't make anything better. He was still Evelyn's pa. Nothing would change that.

I didn't speak for a time. It was Evelyn's turn to talk. Talking with Evelyn was a lot like picking your nose. You had to do a little digging around, but once you hooked a big booger it would slip out like nobody's business.

Sometimes, once you got him started, he'd talk a blue streak. It all depended on his mood.

"He's never going to change, Cammie," said Evelyn.

"Then we've got to make him change. We've got to get down to business. Put our heads together and come up with a good idea." Time was flying by. If we didn't come up with a plan soon, nothing would ever be different. I'd be stuck in Tanner with Aunt Millie, and Evelyn would always be afraid of his pa. That sloop ox he wanted so badly would never show up.

We chewed over different ideas, but nothing sounded right. In the middle of our brain session, Evelyn pulled something out of his pocket. "Ever see a blasting cap?" he asked.

It's not like you can always go by what Evelyn tells you. Where would he get a blasting cap? Knowing that Evelyn likes to run the rig on me from time to time, I had to be sure. Whatever it was he was holding, I could tell it was small.

"It's not very big," I said, viewing it from a nose-length away. I knew what a blasting cap was used for, but I'd never seen one before.

"Don't let the size fool you," said Evelyn with a grin. He made a quick leap toward me and shouted out a loud "Bang!" I screamed and made a jump back, and he laughed.

"Cut that out!" I squawked. A quick punch in the arm was enough to show him I meant business.

"I swiped it from Marcus Pierce the other day when I was helping him out."

"So you stole it." I stated it like a fact. No point asking the obvious. Didn't seem to me like something Evelyn would do. He'd been helping Marcus out on the farm all spring, and I thought they got along pretty good together. Evelyn's old man would grumble that Marcus was taking advantage, but I knew Evelyn was looking for someplace to hang out, away from home, away from his pa. No one could blame him for that.

"Marcus won't even know it's gone. He's got a whole cupboardful in the barn. Besides," he said, "he doesn't use them anymore."

"Maybe there's a reason Marcus doesn't use them— ever think of that? I mean, they are kind of dangerous."

"Only if you're a dummy," laughed Evelyn. I wasn't so sure I wanted anything to do with it. "One of these beauties did the number on Keith's fingers, you know."

Yes, I did know. Everyone in Tanner knew, for that matter. I would've expected Evelyn to take it more serious, seeing as how he was there last fall when Keith McGraw lost those fingers. It happened one day when old man McGraw took Keith with him to blast some stumps in a piece of farmland he was clearing.

Evelyn went out to the McGraw farm that day when he heard the explosions from his place. By the time he got there, Keith had lost his fingers, and his mother was running around like a chicken with its head cut off. Keith's hand was wrapped in bloody bandages. His parents shoved him into the cab of the truck and took off for the doctor with rocks and mud spitting off their tires.

"That's what you get when you let a kid do a man's job," Aunt Millie said at the time. I couldn't help thinking she was right.

Keith ended up losing two months of school on account of it all. People said he was lucky he didn't lose his entire hand. When he came back to school he showed off his missing fingers like he was proud, never mind he could hardly hold a pencil after that.

Evelyn put the blasting cap back in his shirt pocket. "I know, Cammie, let's blow up old Hux's moonshine still!" he said all eager-like.

"Blow up old Hux's still," I said. "Are you serious?"

"We already know where his operation is," he said.

We'd stumbled across Hux's camp last fall when we were exploring the river. It's deep in the woods, but close enough for us to walk; a place where most people would never think to look. When you're running an illegal operation you've got to be cautious. Evelyn knew right away it belonged to Hux Wagner. Who else in Tanner makes moonshine? No one else would dare.

"But how's that going to help *our* situation?" I needed some details. You don't just go around blowing things up for no good reason.

"It's simple. If Hux doesn't have a still, your aunt Millie will be put out of business. That would mean Pa wouldn't have any place handy to buy moonshine," said Evelyn. Things started to make a little sense then.

"And he couldn't go out just any old day of the week to get more," I added. Jim Merry came to our back door about every other night to buy moonshine, and so far as I knew, Aunt Millie was the only bootlegger for miles around.

"Not only that," said Evelyn, "if your aunt Millie didn't make any money selling moonshine…" I could tell where this was all going. That's when I really got excited.

"She couldn't afford to have me around anymore!" I said, grinning from ear to ear.

"Exactly!"

Aunt Millie complained all the time about the cost of things nowadays. What would she do if she had no money coming in? She could kiss those weekly trips to the Clip 'n' Curl goodbye, for starters. I bet the thought of sending me off to Halifax wouldn't sound too shabby to her then.

My hopes soared high for a few moments, but then doubt jabbed me with a quick fist. What if we couldn't pull it off? Plans always sound better when they're in the thinking-up stage. When you stop to consider how you're actually going to make it all happen, it's a whole other story. Would it even be possible to blow up Hux's still? We were just a couple of kids, and this was serious stuff.

Evelyn drew in a quick breath and said, "Come on, Cammie. What have we got to lose?" real excited like it was the best idea he'd ever come up, better than an ice cream cone or a handful of peanuts. I hesitated some more before finally giving in. Evelyn was right. What did we have to lose? Nothing, so far as I could tell.

We went to work figuring out the particulars, the whens, wheres, and hows of it all. When we walked home that day we had a plan in place, one that would get us both what we wanted. Evelyn seemed so confident, so sure our plan would work. I wanted to believe it, too, with all my heart. *This might be our only chance to change our lives,* I thought. Chances like that don't come along every day of the week. As Evelyn turned up the driveway to his place, I stopped him.

"Do you think we can do it?" I asked. A lot was riding on this. If we messed things up I'd be doomed to stay in Tanner, and Evelyn's pa would spend the rest of his days getting drunk and rowdy.

Evelyn smiled real big. "Leave it to me, Cammie," he said. "I won't let you down."

Chapter Thirteen

Hux Wagner's old blue truck sputtered and coughed as it climbed the hill to Aunt Millie's place. It sounded the same way Fred Paper had the day he swallowed a grasshopper on a dare. Puffs of black smoke shot out from the tailpipe and the air stank to high heaven, but the truck kept chugging along like nobody's business. No worries that Hux was going to roll in without everyone in the next county hearing. I could have told Aunt Millie that, but she wouldn't have listened to anything I had to tell her. If something wasn't her idea, she didn't want to hear it at all.

I beat it for the kitchen to tell Aunt Millie that Hux was on the way. She didn't say a thing at first. She kept sipping away at her tea like she had all the time in the world. I didn't stop to think that maybe she wasn't feeling so good after last night.

"Well, get on out there before he takes it in his head to walk right in again," she said waving her arm. Her voice was coarse like rock salt. Most times her words stung like a load of rock salt would, too. Her bleached blonde hair was a bit messy, even I could see that. Usually she didn't have a hair out of place. I guess seeing old Hux wasn't a good enough reason to get fixed up. Might have known she'd be quick enough to rinse out most of the peroxide before it could do too much damage. You'd think she had three arms.

"Don't stand there gawking," she said, setting her teacup down. I could tell she was puckering her face up like a hen's rear end when she spoke. She probably thought I didn't know, but I could tell what she was doing. When I was little I'd sit on her lap when the moonshine was flowing, listening to the goings-on in the kitchen. I'd seen her make that face so many times it got so I didn't even have to look at her. I could hear it in her voice.

I knew there was no point in arguing with her, so I hurried back outside. I wondered what Aunt Millie was thinking, having me wait out on the doorstep for Hux. As loud as what that old truck was, she would have had plenty of time to get out of the house before the wheels stopped rolling. Guess she thought it made her look important if Hux had to be the one waiting for her. That way she would come hurrying out like she was rushed for time when all she was doing was just sitting at the table enjoying a cup of tea.

So I was to keep Hux outside once he arrived, tell him that Her Majesty would be with him in a moment, make sure he didn't walk right in like he did the last time he came to the house. You'd swear he'd never heard tell of knocking. Aunt Millie claimed there were things missing after he left. Knowing her it could have been something as small as a bobby pin she thought she'd set on the hall table.

"Don't you let old Hux touch anything. I don't want him so much as bending down to smell the flowers in the garden." Like Hux sniffing a daisy or two would do her any harm. That had to be one of the most ridiculous things I'd ever heard her say.

The truck sputtered a few more times before Hux cut the switch. If any truck could fart it would be old Hux's. Butch was sitting on the passenger's side, head stuck out the window. I reached in and patted him. His fur was slick and smooth, soft as a baby's bum. His tongue slid out of the corner of his mouth, pink and shiny as a junk of pig's liver. I knew Butch found it hot sitting there in the truck, but he had no say in the matter. That's something Butch and me had in common. I didn't have a say in anything either.

Butch was a black and white bulldog, homely as a stump fence. I didn't hold that against him, though. Butch and me, we've got more in common than the average person might think.

"Hey there, Blind-eyed Cammie, Millie around today?"

I could have hauled off and given him a good clout for calling me Blind-eyed Cammie like that, but it wouldn't have made any difference. He'd laugh it off like it didn't mean a thing. I'd be even more of a joke to him than I already was. That's why I didn't say anything to the kids at school when they teased me, either.

Hux was grinning like a baboon. The dark, round holes where his eyes were told me they might be brown. It was a sure bet I wasn't going to get close enough to see. His hair stuck off in all directions like he'd just woke up from a nap.

"Aunt Millie's in the middle of something, but she's on her way. She said for you to wait." Hux grunted.

"Good boy," I said to Butch, rubbing the top of his head. Butch soaked up the awkward silence like a sponge and I liked that. Nothing like an animal or a little kid to talk to when you can't think of anything much to say.

Butch slobbered over me. Wet drool dripped from his warm tongue. I wiped my hand on my shirt. Since the only way a dog can sweat is through its tongue, I didn't mind Butch's slobber. He couldn't help it. Not in the heat.

"Hot 'nuff fer ya?" asked Hux, pulling out an old red hanky and wiping his forehead.

"Sure is."

"What're they calling fer tamarra?"

I shrugged. Did he think I was the weatherman? If he wanted the forecast, maybe he should have turned on the truck radio—if it even had one, that is. Hux gave his nose a quick swipe with the hanky then lifted his rear end up, and poked the hanky into his back pocket. I continued to pat Butch's head.

Hux blew a quick shot of air through his lips and made a whistling sound as if that was going to make him feel cooler. It was an exaggeration on his part. It was only the end of May.

Head stuck out the window, he let a gob of tobacco spit fly. I could bet Aunt Millie was not going to like Hux Wagner spitting his old tobacco juice out in the dooryard for her to waddle through, but it wasn't up to me to point that out. He rubbed his sleeve against his mouth and chin.

"Good sittin'-in-the-shade kinda weather, if ya ask me."

I knew he was staring, could sense something sitting on his tongue right ready to be spoken. Then it came.

"Something different 'bout you today," he said. "Whatcha got there on your face—new glasses?"

I might have been pleased as punch if someone else had

noticed my new glasses, but having Hux Wagner make mention of them didn't fizz me in the least. I grunted out a yes and looked toward the door, wishing Aunt Millie would hurry.

I could tell Hux was getting a little antsy. He tapped out a tune on the steering wheel.

Shave and a haircut; two bits.

I hated that I was repeating those words in my head while he tapped away.

"I ain't got all day," he finally grumbled. "What's she doing in there? I got customers waiting over in Sheppard Square. Time's money, ya know."

He pushed on the horn with the palm of his hand. *Honk...honk!* The sound fanned outward and echoed down across the hill. Still no sign of Aunt Millie. Like a clucky hen, she couldn't be roused, no way, no how.

"Why don't I just start carrying 'em in fer ya," Hux finally said, yanking on the door handle. Before I knew it, he was out of the truck pulling up the waistband on his trousers. You'd think he'd buy a belt to keep his pants up, or else get some pants with a decent fit. There can't be the money in moonshining like everyone thinks.

I barked out a quick, "No!" and saw old Hux jump. "Aunt Millie said to wait for her here. I don't know where she wants them put. You know what Aunt Millie gets like."

That wasn't a complete lie. Aunt Millie hides the moon-shine somewhere in the house. No one knows exactly where. Not even me. She's not about to get raided and sent off to jail. Knowing Aunt Millie it was probably buried as deep as a pirate's chest.

Hux let out another grunt. "Lord tunderin', that woman could put a businessman in the poorhouse." Yes, I did know, but I didn't much care, not about Hux Wagner and not about his lousy moonshine business. It wouldn't bother my time none if he had to stop his moonshining altogether. As a matter of fact, that would be right up my alley. It would save a lot of work for me and Evelyn.

Hux scrambled onto the back of the truck. There was a supply of crates, each one filled with bottles that clinked together when he moved them about. He set three crates out near the back and jumped down off the truck, real limber. Pretty good for an old-timer.

When the door finally swung open, Aunt Millie ap-peared wearing a million-dollar smile.

"Morning, Hux," she said, like she was falling down surprised at Hux's being there.

"Millie." Hux nodded. The annoyance he'd been feeling a few seconds ago took off like a hayseed in the wind.

Hux got right to work setting the crates of moonshine outside the door.

"Take them inside, Cammie," said Aunt Millie. I knew she didn't want me there while she conducted business.

I opened the door while they discussed the business end of things. I could hear the sound of paper money being pulled from Aunt Millie's pocket. I hesitated, scared to pick up the entire crate, scared of trying to make it inside the house without all those bottles landing on the floor and mashing to smithereens, even more scared of Aunt Millie locking me in my room for the rest of the weekend if I managed to break any of those precious bottles.

"What are you waiting for?" she asked, waving me on my way.

"I'm not waiting for anything," I snapped back. The crate had rope handles on either side. I grabbed fast. My arms buckled, my knees wobbled beneath the hem of my skirt as I lifted it up off the ground. I was sure the crate weighed a ton and a half. I've never been very strong.

"Drop them bottles and you may as well pack up your things," Aunt Millie barked. I rolled my eyes.

"It wouldn't hurt you to help," I said.

"Nonsense. You're just not trying hard enough."

"Here, let me get that," Hux said, stepping into the picture. He sounded annoyed. He took the crate from my scrawny arms. The smell of perspiration whistled past me.

"The girl's no bigger than a minute, Millie. First thing she'll drop the goods and we'll both be out."

"Minute, schminute, she's strong enough when she wants to be," said Aunt Millie.

I shook the hurt out of my arms. The tips of my fingers tingled.

"Just set them down inside the door. We'll take it from here," said Aunt Millie. She waited until Hux had all three crates inside before giving him the money. I removed the bottles and set the empty crates outside. He'd be back in two weeks with another batch. I could almost set my watch by him.

"Nice doing business with ya, Millie," said Hux as he climbed behind the wheel of his truck.

As soon as Hux took off, Aunt Millie gave me a smack upside the head. Even though it didn't hurt, I yelped to keep her from smacking me a second time. Second-time smacks were usually harder. The first time was a hint of more to come if I didn't watch it. Second time I knew she meant business.

As Hux's old truck headed back down the drive, I turned to watch him go.

You'll get yours, Hux Wagner, I thought to myself as his truck turned onto the road. *Evelyn and me, we've got some pretty big plans for that operation of yours. Just you wait.*

Chapter Fourteen

The king and queen must have their own set of spies in the world, people trained to know all the proper ways to snoop. They likely just snap their fingers to get the job done. When you're important in the world you have to be careful. No telling what's waiting around the corner for you. Doesn't matter how much you're loved by the masses, there's bound to be someone out there hateful enough to want to hurt you. Being from England, they're probably on high alert most of the time, with all the countries they've squabbled with over the years. I know it would make me nervous.

I kept thinking about the king and queen that afternoon when we set out for Hux's. I'm not sure why. Maybe it was because I wanted to imagine them doing ordinary things like the rest of us. It didn't seem fair to think that some folks have everything handed over to them while the rest of us have to scrounge for every little thing we get.

It must be nice to have your own set of spies, though. That part I couldn't deny. Evelyn and I only had each other to count on. No amount of finger snapping would tell us what we needed to know. We had to do it ourselves. Right or wrong, we'd get the job done.

We stayed hidden in a clump of bushes upriver from Hux's camp. The leaves were out pretty good, so we didn't have to worry about being seen, not that Hux expected anyone to be spying on him. If time had gone any slower we'd have had to have been riding on a snail's back. It was nothing like the day we went out to Sheppard Square to spy on Mrs. Deveau. That day it was kind of fun, with Evelyn describing everything out to me. Too bad things turned out the way they did. I had to keep telling myself this time would be different.

After the first few hours I decided that the spy world wasn't all it was cracked up to be. I kept asking Evelyn what Hux was doing and Evelyn kept saying, "Nothin'."

It's easy to see that undercover work could put a person to sleep pretty quickly. We had to make sure Hux wasn't anywhere near his precious still when Evelyn threw the blasting cap into the fire. We planned to get rid of the still, not blow up old Hux in the bargain.

"No sense taking chances and messing things up," Evelyn said. I knew what he meant. Sometimes you've got to be patient and wait for the right time.

Watching Hux most of the afternoon made me feel like saying to heck with our whole plan. No way was it going to happen. If it were up to me, I'd have gone home long ago. Evelyn's the one with all the patience. Says it comes from working with the cattle as much as he does. You've got to have patience to work with animals. I started to think Evelyn was going to make us stand there forever, waiting and watching as old Hux stoked the fire and waited for the tiny drops of moonshine to drip through the copper tubing, tasting and tasting again, whistling away while he worked. Too much quiet and I knew I'd fall asleep for sure.

"What's he doing now?"

"Sitting by the fire with his feet up." Good thing I had Evelyn to be my eyes. He said he didn't mind. He'd been doing it all year.

How long could someone sit around watching a fire burn? Making moonshine is one slow process. It must take thousands of drips to fill up even one bottle, which means a lot of time spent doing nothing. Aunt Millie says old Hux is the best moonshiner for miles around, maybe even the whole province. She says he's got a unique recipe, one that's been handed down. His father was a moonshiner and his father before him. I say he should use his talents for something worthwhile, but who cares what Blind-eyed Cammie thinks?

"It's getting late. Maybe we should just come back some other time," I said, hoping Evelyn would agree.

"You chickening out?" The words were jiggling on his tongue. I knew that teasing sound in his voice.

"Of course I'm not chickening out. What do you take me for?" I punched him lightly in the arm. "But I've got to get home. Aunt Millie will start asking questions."

"You're probably right. It doesn't look like old Hux is going anywhere soon. Why doesn't he just step into the camp for even a moment? That's all the time I need to run out there and chuck it in the fire." He sounded disappointed. His dreams of getting his old man sober would have to wait.

"Next time," I said as I followed Evelyn through the woods. I knew he was probably anxious to get this over with. A lot was riding on it for him. Hard to say how soon it would be before his old man got rowdy again. Me, I had until fall.

The river was quiet, holding its breath as we trekked in secrecy, our spying mission nothing more than a lesson in patience. I hurried along. Aunt Millie would complain if I wasn't there when she got home. But I didn't care. People talk about change all the time, but don't do anything about it. I looked toward the battered sunset. At least Evelyn and me were ready and willing to do something about our lives.

Chapter Fifteen

"Cammie, you get yourself down here this minute! Ed'll soon be here and we won't even be ready."

I was busy fixing the bow on my dress and jumped the moment Aunt Millie bellowed. I looked down at my work. The bow was sloppy and limp. The ends were dragging too, but it would have to do. A bellow like that meant she wanted me there on the double, no ifs, ands, or buts about it. Hurrying down the stairs, I waited in the hallway for Her Majesty's keen inspection. I knew she wouldn't be pleased with what she saw. She never was. If I looked the way Aunt Millie did, always dressed to the nines, maybe I'd feel the same way.

Aunt Millie's dress fit her like a smack on the lips— bright red, just like the lipstick she was wearing. Her nails were sporting a coat of fresh paint to match. She'd thought of everything. Today, when she went into town to have her hair styled at the beauty parlour, she came home crowing how Becky Jenkins raved on about the colour. You can't tell me Becky Jenkins doesn't know Aunt Millie douses her hair in peroxide. Anyone up close and personal with that frizzy mop would have to know it's just not natural.

"I thought I told you to wear the dress I bought you the other day," she said. "Can't you just do what I ask for once in your life?"

"Red makes my skin look like milk. You said so once yourself." I knew she'd be half-miffed at me for not putting it on.

"I wanted us to be a matching pair. You never stop to consider my feelings, do you, Cammie?" Her disappointment stuck out like a sore thumb.

Aunt Millie shouldn't have picked that red dress up at the rummage sale the other day without asking me what I thought of it first. If a woman wears red, it means she's loose. It's a shameful colour to wear out in public. Anyone with an ounce of brains wouldn't go flaunting themselves like that. When you live down near the river, people already have their opinions of you. There's no point in doing something to make them talk even more. It doesn't help that they all know who I live with, either. The red dress she bought me was meant as a bribe, to make up for her lying to me about my father, like things could be smoothed over that easily. It was just one of her tricks. I didn't even want to look at it the day she showed me, but she kept clacking away like she didn't even notice my indifference.

Aunt Millie pulled at the lopsided bow I'd made until she was satisfied. When she was through she stood back and scrutinized me all over again.

"Where's your hair ribbon?" she asked. She threw her hands in the air and stood tapping her one foot.

"Hair ribbons are for babies."

"God knows there's plenty of things working against you, but you could at least make a little effort. Show some pride in your appearance. It's about time you started turning some heads. You'll soon be twelve. Boys start noticing girls at this age. Rose Wilkins got married when she was sixteen."

I glared my disapproval, and shut her up quick when I said, "And we all know why that was."

Aunt Millie let out a sigh. Something still didn't meet her approval. "Do you have to wear those glasses, tonight of all nights?"

"Do you have to go out around with that frizzy mop of hair, tonight of all nights?" I mocked. I couldn't help myself.

"Don't get smart with me, young lady. We're going to the dance hall, not the schoolhouse. You won't even need glasses," she said as she made a grab for them. I swatted at her hands and missed.

"I need them to see!" I wailed.

"What's there to see at the dance hall? Besides, they're as thick as the bottom of milk bottles. Do you really think some boy's going to look twice at you with those things stuck fast to your face?

"They'll look soon enough if I fall flat on my face," I said, readjusting the wire frames. I wasn't going to let her get to me.

"Oh, Cammie, stop exaggerating. They don't help out that much and you know it." She stood with her hand outstretched, expecting me to take them off, but I didn't make a move.

"All right, then," she said when she realized I wasn't going to give in. "If you want to ruin your chances and end up spending your days living here with me, then by all means wear the stupid things. You got along just dandy before Miss Muisey-Pants connived to get them for you."

"Well, now I'm getting along even dandier," I said. "I bet if it was your eyesight you'd be singing a different tune."

Aunt Millie made it sound as though she wanted to be rid of me one day, but I knew differently. Just let me mention that school in Halifax and then we'd see what would happen.

Aunt Millie turned her wrist over and checked the time. "It's too late to change your dress now, Ed'll be here any minute. You did this on purpose, Cammie Deveau. Didn't you?" She pulled my jacket down off the rack and handed it to me. I pushed my arms into the sleeves. A hot burst of anger slapped my cheeks.

"Would you stop calling me Cammie Deveau?" The name, the one that I had come to love as a young child, now made me feel like an impostor.

"You're too touchy is all that's wrong with you."

"Touchy? Because you lied to me about who I am?" I buttoned my jacket. She tried to help, but I swatted her hands away.

"What's done is done. I can't very well go back and undo it, now can I? I thought you might like thinking your father came from money. Everyone likes to feel important, don't they? Well, excuse me for trying to make you feel like someone in this world," said Aunt Millie, sounding as if her feelings were hurt. No sense pointing out the fact that the lie she'd conjured was a bit more elaborate than her telling me my father was Charles Deveau. She didn't even know the Deveaus. All she did was pick the richest family she knew and told me it was mine because she didn't think I'd ever find out the truth. But I could talk myself blue in the face and I wouldn't get her to admit she'd done wrong.

Aunt Millie wrapped a throw over her shoulders. I recognized the rhinestone necklace Drew had given her dangling around her neck. After she and Drew broke up I snuck into her room a few times and put the necklace on. I'd stand in front of the mirror imagining I was the queen wearing the crown jewels.

"I hope we're not staying too late," I said, wishing Ed would show up so that we could get on with it.

"Oh, it's Saturday night, for goodness' sake. Have a little fun. Kick up your heels. Ed was nice enough to invite us."

"Invite you, you mean."

We hadn't seen Ed for a few weeks. But that was nothing unusual. These past ten months I'd become used to him disappearing for weeks or even months at a time. Here today, gone tomorrow. Everyone's got their reasons for the things they do. Sometimes I'd get curious, though, and ask Aunt Millie about him. Her answers came out vague. "Ed's trying to pull himself together," she'd say, or "I'm not sure where Ed's living now. I didn't think to ask."

Then before I knew it he'd be sitting at Aunt Millie's kitchen table when I got home from school. I always figured she knew more than she let on, but Aunt Millie only talked about the things she wanted to. I didn't mind those times when Ed was around. He was laid back. He didn't even get worked up the time I broke the mirror off his truck. And he usually brought me candy when he came for a visit.

"Ed's got restless shoes. I think his head got mixed up in the war," Aunt Millie liked to say. She never seemed upset if the days or weeks went by without a peep from him. If there was any loving going on between them, I never saw any evidence.

I wasn't sure how much fun Aunt Millie thought I was going to have sitting on a chair while she twirled around the dance floor, but I could guarantee it was going to get kind of boring after the first hour or so. Even so, it beat staying home by myself at night, wondering if someone was going to come knocking at the door looking to buy some moonshine.

Aunt Millie did her last-minute primping thing in front the mirror, tilting her head from one side to the other. Satisfied, she opened the clasp on her purse and pulled out a small bottle. I knew it was vanilla extract even before I smelled it. Two daubs behind each ear, a quick tip to her lips, and she closed her purse with a snap.

"People are going to smell that on your breath, you know."

"Oh, who cares what people think? I'm only going around this world once, and I plan on having a good time while I'm at it."

While we were standing by the front door waiting for Ed's truck to drive in, there came a loud banging at the back door.

"Open up, Millie. Open the door!" someone yelled.

Aunt Millie let out a heavy sigh. "Oh, for the love of moonshine!" she said in a whispery voice. She started toward the kitchen, then stood still, as if hoping whoever it was would go away. The door rattled again. Then came a series of thumps that were so loud I swore the door was going to come off its hinges.

"All right, all right, I'm coming," said Aunt Millie. Her high heels clicked against the floor as she hurried toward the back door. I was in hot pursuit, curious myself by that time. The voice on the other side of the door grew louder.

"Hold your horses...Who's out there?" she asked, speaking through the door while at the same time fumbling with the hook.

"It's Jim Merry!" came the crusty reply.

A curse word shot out of Aunt Millie's mouth like a hot coal spitting out of a fire.

"What do you want?" The hook released and the door swung open. Aunt Millie never hid her dislike for Jim Merry.

"I'll take a bottle of Hux's finest," said Jim stepping inside without an invitation.

"I'm just about to leave," she said. The sound of Jim's

change jingling told me she'd give in, though.

"One bottle'll hold me. Make it quick. I got things to do," he said. One thing you never saw on a Saturday night at Aunt Millie's was Jim Merry sitting around the table with the rest of gang. She'd get him a bottle and send him on his way. But the truth is, I don't think Jim was interested in Aunt Millie's company at all. I don't think he liked her any more than she liked him.

Aunt Millie slipped off to her special hiding place to get a bottle, leaving me alone in the kitchen with Jim. He looked over at me.

"You're all dressed up," he said after a few moments of gawking in my direction. "Where're you off to?"

"Sheppard Square," I said, wishing Aunt Millie would hurry. I shifted uncomfortably.

"Going to the big dance, I suppose?"

I nodded.

"Watch yourself when you're over there. Them Sheppard Square boys are a rough bunch. They'll cause trouble sooner than look at you," he said, like he was making it his business to look out for me now that he'd saved my life. He was probably looking for me to say thank you about that day at the river. It would be the only decent thing for me to do. Only how do you say thanks to a man who treats your best friend like dirt?

Before I had time to think up something to say, Aunt Millie walked in. I never thought I'd be happy to see Aunt Millie in the kitchen with a bottle of moonshine in her hands. It took a few seconds for the transaction to take place and for Jim Merry to be on his way.

"Good riddance," she whispered as the door closed behind him.

"Why do you do it?" I asked as she hooked the door. It seemed to me if she had such a hate on for Jim she wouldn't bother doing business with him at all.

"Do what?"

"Sell him moonshine." Life would be a whole lot better for Evelyn if she didn't. Not that she'd give a care about Evelyn.

"Oh, Cammie, just because you've got to be cautious around a certain individual doesn't mean you shouldn't conduct business with him. Lowlife or not, he's one of my best customers." I shook my head. Money was all she cared about.

When a horn honked outside, Aunt Millie looked at me and smiled.

"There's Ed," she said, grabbing hold of my hand. As she whisked me out toward the front door I caught a quick whiff of vanilla extract in the air, a thin, sweet fragrance that lingered in my nostrils, ordering me to follow.

Chapter Sixteen

Being squished between Ed and Aunt Millie didn't make a whole bunch of sense, there being oceans of room on the back of Ed's truck for me to sit. I thought it might be kind of fun sitting out in the open air with the wind messing my hair around, a little bit of time all to myself without Ed or Aunt Millie jabbering back and forth, but I had no say in the matter.

"I'll get on back," I said when Aunt Millie opened the truck door.

"Like heck you will," she said, shoving me in the cab like a sack of old potatoes.

Those two daubs of vanilla extract behind Aunt Millie's ears were no match for Ed's smelly perfume. At least if I had been sitting on back I'd have been able to breathe some fresh air into my lungs. But there was no way for me to get out from between them until the wheels stopped rolling. I felt like a sardine in a can.

"Can you at least turn down your window?" I asked Ed. Aunt Millie gave me a quick poke in the ribs. She knew what I meant, even if Ed didn't.

I caught sight of a cigarette dangling from Ed's lips, waiting to be lit. He pulled a matchbox from out of his shirt pocket, and told me to take one out for him. My fingers fumbled. I could hardly see in the dim lighting without holding the box up close, and even that didn't do much good. It didn't help that the truck was bouncing all over the road.

Finally Ed turned on the interior light, but not before some of the matches went flying into the air. Aunt Millie scooped them up off my lap and shoved them into the box—smooth and fast, like she'd been practising all day. She passed one over to Ed.

There was a quick little crack when Ed flicked the match with his thumbnail. The smell of brimstone replaced the odour of his aftershave for a split second before it fizzled away. He cupped his hands around the flames and tried to light it without taking his hands off the steering wheel. I kept wishing he'd hurry the heck up and get the stupid thing lit before we ran off the road, him all hunched over the way he was.

"Here, take the wheel," he finally said when he couldn't manage to light it. He blew the match out before it burned down to nothing. I reached over and took the wheel. Then came the sound of another match being taken out. This time Ed scratched it across the box.

The steering wheel felt queer in my hands, but in a kick-your-heels-up kind of way.

Me, driving down a summer road in the middle of the day with the windows rolled down, wind blowing through my hair, it tickling my face. Not a care in this whole wide world. I don't even remember Aunt Millie's name and Tanner's not even on my map.

I kept the truck nice and steady while Ed lit his cigarette. My hands held firm to the wheel while he tossed the burnt match out the window. I looked over at him, expecting him to take over. He kept smiling at me so I didn't kick up a fuss, figured it was probably the only chance I'd ever get to steer a vehicle.

It was hard to see where I was headed, but so long as the truck was going forward I knew I was doing fine. Driving wasn't something I ever thought I'd get to do. Well, technically I was just steering, but steering is the biggest part. Having my foot on the gas and brake didn't seem near as important as showing the truck which way it had to go. My heart was happily singing as we drove along. *Look at you, Cammie. Just look at you!* The dark forms of the trees loomed eerily in the shadows on either side of the road and there was me, smug as all get out, thumbing my nose at them all.

"Keep her between the ditches, Cammie," Aunt Millie squealed. I turned my head and looked over to where she was sitting—kind of wondering if she thought I was doing pretty good for myself—when all of a sudden Ed stepped on the gas. The truck made a mad surge ahead. It was fun at first and I laughed out loud—we all did—until the truck hit a humungous pothole in the road. The steering wheel jumped out of my hands and the truck made a wild lunge toward the ditch. I give a loud holler and grabbed tight to the wheel.

"Take it. Take the wheel!" I begged Ed, who was sitting there snickering like a fool. I would have slapped him in the head if it didn't mean I'd have to take my hands off the wheel.

"Help me!" I ordered.

"Calm down, Cammie. Don't get your drawers all twisted," he said. By the time he got around to taking the steering wheel it was too late. The wheels on the passenger's side had dropped down off the side of the road. I bumped into Aunt Millie. She bumped into the door. Ed gave the truck an extra shot of gas and a big twist on the wheel. The truck stopped moving ahead. We were anchored!

Right away, Aunt Millie got ugly about it. "So much for

us going to the dance. Ed, you should have known better. It's not like Cammie can do regular things like the rest of us. Birds can't fly with broken wings." Her words stung like a scraped knee, but I kept my mouth shut. What do you say when someone's speaking the truth?

"Now just stay calm while I survey the situation," Ed said. With the truck cocked up in the air, he could barely manage to scramble out the door. As he walked around outside I heard him say something about putting some rocks under the wheel.

"Great!" I said. "We'll end up walking home." I shouldn't have come. I should have stayed at home and taken my chances. Ed would likely be angry with me for running us off the road. Aunt Millie certainly was. Why was I always messing things up?

Aunt Millie took out her compact and gave her nose one quick daub with the puff.

"Just sit quiet and see what happens," she said, suddenly more concerned about a shiny spot on her nose than the fact that we were hung up high and dry. "Look—here comes help," she said, dropping her compact into her purse. She sounded mighty confident that the people in the vehicle heading our way would help out. When it slowed to a stop, she crawled over me, pushing and shoving her way out the door.

"You stay here," she said as she went to join Ed.

The breeze sent their laughter and voices sprawling into the cool evening air. Did I even have a right to feel left out? Seemed like I was always on the outside; why should it be any different now?

"Millie, you take the wheel and we'll all push," I heard Ed say once they had talked the situation over and decided what to do.

Feet shuffled in the dirt. I don't know how many there were, but it sounded like a herd of cattle passing by. Aunt Millie got back in the truck. When I complained that she elbowed me in the face, she told me to never mind.

"I'm trying to fix up your mess," she said.

I'd never seen Aunt Millie behind the wheel before. Her elbows were bent, her head set in serious style. She looked foolish, if I must say so. If I hadn't been so hurt I might have laughed, her making out she knew what she was doing. Ed hollered out his instructions.

"I got it!" she yelled, her head stuck out the window. Ed counted to three. Aunt Millie stepped on the gas. The tires kicked up rocks and mud. Men were grunting and shouting.

"Keep going…keep going," yelled Ed. Slowly the truck started to move ahead.

"Cut the wheel a bit more!"

Aunt Mille reefed on it.

"More…!"

Again she turned the steering wheel and pushed on the gas.

You'd have thought someone had won the pie-eating contest at the New Ross fair from the hoots and hollers the men let out when the truck came out of the ditch. When Ed got back in the truck, he was all smiles.

"Shaping up to be an interesting evening," he said. I breathed a sigh of relief. Maybe Ed wouldn't hate me after all. We continued on our way as if nothing had happened.

"Were you trying to break the speed limit back there, Ed Hanover? You know Cammie's blind," said Aunt Millie, both hands clamped fast to her purse. That time I jabbed *her* in the ribs. She knew full well I didn't want to be called blind. Most times she wouldn't say it, but when it suited her purpose she slathered the word around like cake frosting. The clasp on her purse snapped. The smell of fresh powder reached my nostrils. She was smiling. I could tell without even looking her way.

"Admit it, you were always one for cheap thrills, Millie Turple," Ed joked. "You'd pay big money for a ride like that at the exhibition. Well, there you got one for free. Didn't she, Cammie?"

At least we wouldn't get killed on the merry-go-round, I

stopped myself from saying out loud. I couldn't be mean to Ed. At least he wasn't blaming me for any of this.

Chapter Seventeen

Aunt Millie and Ed stood outside the dance hall, socializing with some of the locals. My sight may be bad, but I knew what was going on. Aunt Millie was bringing her hand up to her mouth. I knew it meant she had a cigarette stuck between her fingers. A bottle of something was in the other. She never smoked unless she was at a dance. I caught sight of her tossing the butt on the ground and grinding it into the ground with her shoe.

"Come on, Cammie, let's go kick up Jack before this thing closes down," Aunt Millie said, looping her arm in mine. She unwrapped a chew of gum and shoved it in her mouth when I complained about the smell on her breath.

"You want some?" she asked, chomping away like a cow grinding its cud.

The noise inside the dance hall was confusing. Voices came from all around, voices without any faces, without any hint as to who they belonged to. I wanted to crawl off, to get away from the confusion. Instead, we continued to squeeze through the crowd. I gripped fast to Aunt Millie. She looked around until she found a couple of empty chairs. Dropping her purse beside me, she told me to plunk my rear end down.

"And don't go running off," she warned, like I was ever going to do that in a crowd of strangers. Where would I go all by myself?

The fiddler rubbed his bow across the strings, and it sounded just like a cat caught by the tail. Slowly I began to make out some notes, strong, like he was filled with confidence after those first awkward attempts. People headed out onto the dance floor. There was a pause while everyone found a place, before the music started up again. It wasn't hard to see that red dress of Aunt Millie's out on the dance floor, spinning and twirling up a storm. You don't need good eyesight to see a loose woman in action. Hands were clapping in time to the music, feet were stomping, people laughing. I sat there by myself wishing I was a hundred miles from there.

At first I wasn't sure who the women sitting behind me were talking about. I had my attention on the music, the clapping of hands, the feet that were stomping, taking it all in.

"Do you see what that one's wearing?"

"Would you expect anything different?"

There was a lull in the conversation. Out on the dance floor a burst of laughter rose above the music. Aunt Millie. There was no doubt about it.

"Did you see that?"

"If I was Jill Hurshman I'd keep an eye on that situation."

"You'd swear they were old friends. Wouldn't you?"

"I wonder where Floyd Hurshman's been spending *his* Saturday nights."

The three of them were having quite a spree for themselves, making their speculations. I could have told them a thing or two about Floyd Hurshman, shut them up but good. Except I didn't know who Floyd Hurshman was. Might be he's from Tanner, then again he might be from Sheppard Square.

"You want to dance?"

I didn't even notice Ed take the seat next to me. The red dress was still out on the dance floor having a good time. Aunt Millie must have ditched him for someone else. I looked over at Ed, wondering if he was really serious about wanting to dance or if he was taking pity on me sitting there by myself. Ed was too soft for his own good. Even Aunt Millie said so. I wouldn't know what to do on the dance floor. Ed should have known better. Besides, I didn't feel much like dancing.

"You seem down in the dumps," he said. "Something the matter?"

It felt strange, someone asking me how I was feeling. What would be the point in discussing my troubles? Unless, of course, *he* could tell me what I wanted to know. I sat up at attention.

No sense beating around the bush. Might as well spit it out.

"Do you know who my father is?" I asked.

Ed shifted in his seat and rubbed the back of his neck, a move I'd seen him do whenever Aunt Millie and I were having one of our spats.

"What does Millie say?"

"That's just it. It's some big secret. She says I don't need to know. Like it's not even important."

"She probably has her reasons…people usually do."

"Yeah, reasons," I grunted. Ed was sidestepping my question. He wasn't any better than Aunt Millie. Why was everyone so scared of her? She's not even that big.

"Why the sudden interest?" he asked. I wasn't going into that whole lie of Aunt Millie's. It sounded too stupid now. Me thinking I was related to some rich people over in Sheppard Square—as if.

"I was hoping I'd get to go to blind school in Halifax. Maybe my father would say okay just to get me out of his hair." I gathered up all the sarcasm I could muster. I didn't dare hope that he'd actually be glad to know me. Who'd want me, anyway? So long as I got a new life, would I even need to get to know my father?

Ed cleared his throat. "Isn't that up to Millie? I mean, the blind school. You might get homesick. Halifax is a long ways away."

Great. Why did I expect him to understand?

"Believe me, it's not far enough," I said.

I should have known better than to ask. How would Ed know who my father was? He'd spent all those war years away. I thought maybe he'd heard some gossip was all. Maybe it was a lost cause. I'd never learn the truth. Maybe nothing would ever change. Could be I'd spent my life hoping for the impossible.

"Come on, Cammie. You don't really mean that. I know Millie has her ways, but still," he said rubbing the back of his neck again. Of course he'd say that. Aunt Millie was usually on her best behaviour when he was around. Anyway, my questions must have got the best of him because he didn't stick around for long.

"I'm going out for a smoke," he said. "Will you be okay here by yourself?"

I nodded. Of course I'd be okay.

When the music finally stopped and someone announced that it was time to take a break, the red dress pushed its way through the crowd, bringing Aunt Millie with it.

"Drew and I are stepping outside for a few minutes, Cammie. You stay here," she said, grabbing her purse.

"Drew? Don't tell me—" I started to say.

"Just never you mind," she said, wrapping her throw around her shoulders. "We've got some things to talk over, is all."

People shuffled toward the doorway. I wanted to follow but didn't have the courage. I knew if I got up off my seat I'd never find it again. I sat swinging my legs back and forth, the ugliest duckling in the entire lake. At least with the music playing I hadn't felt so all alone.

The heat in the dance hall was almost unbearable. I looked at the empty chairs around me. There were a few people sitting here and there, but most of the chairs were empty. The women who'd been sitting behind me had disappeared. Good riddance to bad rubbish.

I pried my bare legs loose from the chair, stood up to stretch, and pulled my dress down over my knees. What could Aunt Millie be thinking about, talking to Drew Bordmann again? Had she forgotten all the fights they'd had? I paced in front of my chair, without the courage to venture very far. Dread grabbed me by the toes and hauled me down through the floorboards. I mulled over the idea that maybe she and Drew would get back together again. Someone had to put a stop to that. I didn't want that someone to be me. I wished there was some small space to crawl into, to hide myself away. When you're just one person, even in a whole crowd of many, no one even knows you're alive.

Chapter Eighteen

The moment someone yelled that a fight was about to start outside, I was on my feet. A knot bunched up in the pit of my stomach like a sun-dried raisin. I'd seen my share of fights, and near fights, at the house, and I couldn't imagine anyone else out there tonight was as feisty as Aunt Millie, right ready to pounce at the least provocation. No way a fight was going to happen without her being caught in the middle of it all, that much I knew.

I tried to recall which way we'd come in, turning about worse than a bat flying in daylight. Why did Aunt Millie always abandon me, walk away without saying a word? This wasn't the first time. She took me to the New Ross fair last year and disappeared. I cried and wailed until a man asked me what was wrong. When I told him that Aunt Millie was gone and I didn't know where, he sat me on a bench and told me to stay put.

"Don't you ever send someone after me again, Cammie Deveau," Aunt Millie said when she finally showed up. "It's not like I wasn't going to come back for you. This is New Ross, for goodness' sake. Even a blind person couldn't get lost in New Ross." I clung to her arm for the rest of the afternoon. Actually, that was the night Drew Bordmann took us home and ended up staying for months.

Fear swept me off my feet. I stopped for a moment to calm down my insides, and took a few deep breaths. I could do this. No cause to panic. I could get myself outside, find Aunt Millie, and tell her it was time to go home.

Common sense gave me a quick poke. A cool stream of air touched my cheek—the door was to my left. The breeze would show me the way out. People were clinging to the doorway like mosquitoes to a screened-in porch. I pushed my way though the shoulders and heads, and stood out on the steps. The sky was pitch black like when you close your eyes at night. I knew the tiny bits of light in the sky were stars. The moon was a silver smear, like maybe God spit on his thumb and smudged it just a little. Crickets sent shrill, sharp songs into the night. Could they sense that something was in the works? I should have figured it couldn't be as simple as us going to a dance and coming home.

June bugs pinged against the outside light. One

whooshed at me and I ducked out of the way. The bulb didn't make much of a light. I couldn't see anything past the bottom step, but there was nothing wrong with my hearing. Swear words were exploding into the air like shooting stars. If I were a true lady, like Miss Muise, I would have been shocked. But I grew up on swear words, swallowed them down like cod-liver oil.

I grabbed the handrail and made my way to the bottom, gingerly feeling for each step. People were camped out on the steps, some of them smoking cigarettes, all of them waiting for some juicy morsel to be thrown their way. I felt like running the toe of my shoe up their rear ends and telling them to go find something else to do.

If it wasn't for Aunt Millie being out there I would have stayed in the hall where she'd left me. But a nagging inside urged me onward, like someone poking me from behind with a stick.

Curse words continued to be bounced around like a rubber ball. The voices were coming from behind the dance hall. Aunt Millie's voice spiralled above the rest. It sounded as though she'd crawled inside a tin can that got kicked into outer space. I didn't know what I could do, I just knew I couldn't stand there and do nothing. I forgot myself and started to hurry, making a sudden stab in the dark. The ground was uneven and I began to lose my balance. Someone grabbed me by the arm and steadied me before I fell flat on my face.

"What are you doing out here, Cammie?" It was Ed.

"Where is she? Can you take me to her?" Aunt Millie was saying some pretty nasty things. Trouble was brewing. I didn't have to be a genius to figure that out. "Do something, Ed. We can't just stand here."

"You shouldn't be out here, Cammie. Let me take you inside. It's not safe."

Because I'm half-blind! I wanted to scream, but I didn't. Right now I needed Ed's help more than I needed to stick up for myself.

"That's it, is it, Millie? You got Drew to fight your battles for you tonight because Ed's nothing but a coward?" someone shouted. I felt a sudden embarrassment for Ed, but quickly reminded myself that no one out there would remember what was said come morning.

Laughter followed, a whole string of it, so full, so rich that it covered up what Aunt Millie had to say. If we were at the house, things would be different. At the house Aunt Millie's boss, but in Sheppard Square she's just plain old Millie Turple, a bigmouth and a troublemaker. They're not scared of her.

"I can tell you that I don't need Drew Bordmann or anyone else butting into my business," Aunt Millie shouted. I knew the fists were soon going to fly. There would be black eyes and bruises come morning.

"Just take me to Aunt Millie," I insisted, looking up at Ed.

"This is close enough, Cammie, really. I'll go get her. It's time we went home anyway. You stay here," said Ed.

Darkness or no darkness, if Ed Hanover thought I was going to stand out there by myself while he got in on all the action, he was dead wrong. As soon as his back was turned, I took off.

One thing I have learned from my years with Aunt Millie is that if I don't figure out a way to do something on my own, no one will do it for me. I charged through the crowd, pushing when they refused to budge.

"Get out of here, Cammie!" cried Aunt Millie when I eventually broke through the pack. I hurried toward the sound of her voice, relieved to have found her in the crowd.

"I told you to stay put," Ed scolded. He was clearly annoyed with me.

"I never said I was staying," I told him before grabbing Aunt Millie by the arm. "Can't we go now?" I asked her.

She stiffened her legs like a spoiled kid who doesn't want to move. I pulled on her arm, but she wouldn't budge.

"Millie, listen to Cammie. Let's just call it a night," said Ed, taking her by the other arm. For a wonder, she began to move.

"Come on back, Millie. You going to let that blind girl lead you?" someone in the crowd yelled out. She stopped in her tracks.

I recognized Drew Bordmann's voice, that gravelly rumble I despised for all those months he hung around at the house.

"The blind leading the blind!" someone repeated with a laugh. A big welt of humiliation slapped my face, leaving an ugly red mark behind. I felt like crawling under a rock, but I couldn't. I had to gather up Aunt Millie and get her out of there. I couldn't do that if I was off soothing my hurt feelings. So I did the best thing I could think of.

"You come with us or I'll have you reported," I said sounding as tough as I could. I wanted her to know I meant business, and I didn't have all night to do it. She wasn't about to run the risk of maybe going to jail or paying a big fine.

"You wouldn't dare," she snapped.

"Don't think so?" In her present state she might actually believe I would report her for selling moonshine.

"I always said you'd turn on me one day, Cammie Deveau. I didn't think it would be tonight."

"Are you coming?"

"Fine then, it's not worth fighting over," she said as we started to walk past the onlookers. I looked straight ahead, pretending not to know they were watching, which they most surely were.

"The night's still young, Millie," Drew called out above the hum of voices.

"Slow down, Cammie," Aunt Millie protested as we weaved a crooked trail among the people, with Ed in the lead. "Wait a minute. I'm not through here. I've got something more to say."

She spun back toward the crowd and accidentally hit my nose with her arm. My glasses went flying. I wasn't sure what to do, which way to turn. I only knew I had to get them back! I fell down on my knees, my nose throbbing as I felt around in the dark.

Aunt Millie started shouting out that she wanted to go home; she'd had enough. Panic swelled inside me. My glasses had to be somewhere. They couldn't have gone too far. We couldn't leave until I found them.

Gravel and rocks bit my palms. Dirt pushed beneath my fingernails as I searched the ground. Aunt Millie was in a tear to leave. There wasn't much time. I had to find them!

"Get up from down there, Cammie Deveau," Aunt Mille ordered like she had suddenly been put in charge of the world again.

"My glasses!" I cried. A squeaky note of desperation escaped my throat. How in the world would I find them in the dark? Her red high-heeled shoes stepped on my fingers. "Get off my hand and stop standing in the way," I hissed. None of this would have happened if she had acted like any decent person would. I made a swat at her but missed.

"Didn't I tell you to keep those stupid things at home? Oh, for pity's sake…Ed, get over here and help Cammie find her eyeglasses."

"Make room," someone from the crowd yelled as we continued to scrounge around the ground like kids at a peanut scramble. There was a pause. Everyone was waiting. Would there be a fight or wouldn't there? In that brief moment it wasn't completely clear. Then came the sound of feet shuffling against the gravel.

I'm not sure who threw the first punch or why, I only know that the moment before it happened I was surrounded by a stampede of feet, people trying to get out of the way. I jumped to my feet to avoid being trampled. I knew I might as well kiss my eyeglasses goodbye.

I could sense the tension, taste the fear—it was as thick as jelly but not at all sweet. Aunt Millie grabbed me. I had no idea where Ed had parked the truck but I was willing to follow wherever she led me so long as it was some place safe. I was half-running, half-stumbling, half-whining about my lost eyeglasses when she shook me off.

"Stop whining, Cammie. There's nothing we can do about it now," she said as she opened the truck door and shoved me inside.

"What's going on?" I asked, confused, as I realized the person sitting behind the wheel wasn't Ed. Even without my glasses I could tell that much. Aunt Millie didn't answer.

"We're not in the right truck," I said as a sick feeling struck me in the pit of my stomach.

"What's the matter, Cammie? Won't I do?"

I cringed at the sound of the voice next to me. On the trip home Aunt Millie nattered away without a care in the world, never mind she was the one responsible for my lost eyeglasses, never mind she'd probably caused the whole racket outside the dance hall. The clasp on her purse made a quick snap, and I could smell vanilla extract. I closed my eyes and wished with all my strength that this was not my life.

Chapter Nineteen

Aunt Millie grabbed fast to my arm as she stumbled her way toward the front door.

"Hang on a minute," she said, and bent down to straighten the seams on the back of her nylon stockings. They had probably been as crooked and coiled as a snake all evening. Why be bothered about them now?

I had fumed all the way home, my blood boiling inside my veins. I was waiting to get Aunt Millie alone so that I could have it out with her, maybe make her go back for my glasses in the morning. If they were even there to be found. The fact that Drew Bordmann took us home was like rubbing iodine in the wound.

Beneath the bright light of Drew's headlights we managed our way up the footpath without falling flat on our faces. Without my glasses, I felt naked. I'd only had them a few weeks, but already they were a part of me. If I didn't get them back, my world would be all fuzzy again. In the dark I could pretend nothing much had changed, but when daylight came it would be a different story. I held back tears as we walked along. I could make out where the front door was and I steered Aunt Millie toward it. She was muckled fast to my arm like I was a greased pole at the fair. With exaggerated steps, she brought her feet down one at a time. We must have looked the stylish pair, making our way along. Good thing we had no handy neighbours standing back watching it all unfold. We'd end up being the topic of conversation for days to come, but then I was pretty sure everyone would be talking about this night anyway. I should be used to it by now, and you'd almost think I would be, but it's tough knowing that people are whispering about your life. Aunt Millie mightn't be much, but she's all I've got. When you're stripped down naked, having a dirty old rag to wear is better than nothing.

Before we reached the doorstep, Drew hollered out something from the truck. We turned around, dazzled by the bright headlights.

"Turn those things down, would you?" Aunt Millie hollered out. Drew dimmed the headlights and cut the engine. The truck clattered to a complete stop. For a few moments it was as if all sound had been drained from the night. With a long, thin arm the night air fanned the treetops.

The leaves trembled overhead. I knew the stillness would be short-lived. There was no way it could survive. People like Drew and Aunt Millie don't notice such things. Maybe I'm the only one in Tanner who does.

Drew climbed out of the truck, ready to rush to Aunt Millie's aid the second she gave the word. He probably had ideas of coming in for the night.

"I said, do you want me to unlock the door for you?" Drew bellowed louder this time. I was certain they could hear him all the way in Sheppard Square. A dog began barking off in the distance. I thought it must be that mangy mutt of Otis Tanner's, the one that runs loose around the neighbourhood at night. It sure didn't sound like Buster, the Merrys' hound.

"Listen, knucklehead, since when do I need a man to unlock a door for me?" Aunt Millie yelled out. Her words, as fresh as the night breeze, came out scattered and whipped. I knew they would be forgotten the moment she uttered them.

"Just leave your low beams on so we can see to get in," she said, turning back toward the house. She jabbed me with her elbow. "Stop gawking at Drew and help me with the door."

We stepped up onto the doorstep. Fumbling inside her purse, she pulled out the key. Most folks around don't lock their doors when they go away. Then again, most folks around don't keep hoardes of moonshine hidden in their houses. Aunt Millie worked the key into the padlock and gave it a twist. She slipped it off and put it in her purse. Drew started up his old jalopy and backed down the driveway. I was glad she hadn't invited him in. Maybe she realized I'd have kicked up a stink if she had.

We opened the front door. The house was full of shadows. I used to be frightened of the shadows when I was small, the whispered voices I heard coming from across the hall in the middle of the night, Aunt Millie's soft, throaty laughs that spiralled like a bird in flight. In the morning there'd be a man sitting at the kitchen table, Aunt Millie flitting about like a feather in the wind, fixing him a hearty breakfast and then sending him on his way. The next month there would be someone new sitting at the table.

I was still angrier than a nest of stirred-up hornets at the both of them. If it hadn't been for them I would never have lost my glasses. What was I going to do? More importantly, what would I tell Miss Muise? She'd be sure to notice my missing glasses. She picked up on things like that, unlike Aunt Millie, who wouldn't notice if I sprouted a set of horns until she planned on taking me out in public with her. I could imagine the disappointment that was bound to be in Miss Muise's voice. Why did I always have to ruin everything?

"There was no need to take your glasses in the first place. You never listen to someone who knows a little something. You were bullheaded right from the time you were born. Just like Brenda," Aunt Millie said.

I felt for the light switch just inside the door. "Leave my mother out of this," I said. How dare she criticize my mother after all the lies she'd told? Sometimes even I was surprised by Aunt Millie's nerve.

Before I reached the switch, a crash came from out in the kitchen. I froze like a statue. "Someone's in here," I whispered.

"I know that!" she snapped. "Now hush."

Feet shuffled from one end of the kitchen to the other. It sounded as though someone was ransacking the place. A man brandished a whole string of curse words that ran together like broken egg yolks in a mixing bowl. There was another series of sounds; tinny, like someone rummaging through the pots and pans. What could he be looking for?

Fear trickled through me like the swig of apple cider I had last Christmas.

I wanted to run out the front door as fast as I could. I wanted to leave Aunt Millie standing there by herself and never turn back. If I had had someplace to go, you can bet I'd have been gone. If I could see better, I could have left and got along all on my own. But I lost out on both counts.

In a cat's wink, Aunt Millie was alert and ready to pounce. She pushed her purse at me and ordered me to hand her something. I wasn't sure what she meant by "something." I handed her the only thing I could think of, the poker from the parlour stove. She grabbed it and raised it above her head. I stuck close behind.

"Got to be here someplace." The voice was familiar, but still I couldn't place it. Maybe it was because my heart was beating like crazy in my chest. Turning the doorknob, Aunt Millie opened the kitchen door with a kick and a grunt. A cool breeze streamed out from the kitchen. I knew the back door was wide open. But how? I'd heard Aunt Millie hook it after Jim Merry left earlier in the evening. Light from the living room illuminated the kitchen, but not enough for me to get a look inside. Someone was in the shadows. I could hear breathing, hard and full of anger.

"Who's in here?" Aunt Millie demanded. "Come out with you." Her voice was brittle, hard as rock candy. We waited a few moments for someone to speak up. Nothing.

"Hit the switch," she said, like it was going to happen all slick just because she gave me the order. Shaking, I felt like I'd been plunged into ice water. I'd never felt so cold before, not even that day out in the river when I nearly drowned.

I made a few wild stabs for the switch. My hand hit the wall frantically, fear building inside me. Someone grabbed my arm and I yelled out.

"Get over here!" a man cried as he pulled me toward him. Pots and pans clattered beneath my feet. I pushed a scream up from the bottom of my toes. I didn't hold anything back. I screeched like it was the last noise I was ever going to make, all the while my final demise playing out in my mind.

Me, lying cold on the floor, the worst fate that could have ever befallen me. So much for the new life I'd been wanting all this time, all the work, all the planning to get myself off to blind school. I could kiss it all goodbye. Aunt Millie showing some concern for the first time in my life and me, stone cold dead, not knowing a thing about it. Me, lying in my coffin with the gang standing around with their heads hung low, the sorriest-looking bunch you'd ever want to see.

A hot, sweaty hand clamped over my mouth. Moonshine first and then perspiration, the smells creating an offensive recipe. Afraid to wriggle free, I stood pressed against his chest. Aunt Millie continued to sputter about not being able to find the light switch. *Just hurry up and do something,* my mind shouted.

"Where's your moonshine?" the voice in the dark asked. I knew that voice. It was Jim Merry!

Aunt Millie slapped at the wall in search of the switch until, like magic, the light came on. She was standing in the doorway with the poker raised above her head.

"Get your hands off Cammie! This has nothing to do with her." Her voice took a bite out of the room. I wondered if he'd do as she ordered.

"I'm not meaning to hurt anyone. I just want a little something to drink," he said.

"I sold you a bottle already tonight," she shot back.

"Yeah, well, I don't have it anymore." They continued to argue back and forth, Jim with his hand clamped over my mouth. I could scarcely breathe. I squirmed to get away as his arm tightened across my throat.

"I'm not leaving until I get what I want," Jim finally said.

"Well you're out of luck, Jim Merry, because that was my last bottle. Hux isn't due until tomorrow. He's a little late this time around." I knew it was soon time for Hux to put in an appearance, but surely she wasn't completely out. Surely she could scrounge up something to satisfy him. And surely this was no time for her to be telling another one of her lies.

"What if I take the little blind girl with me as collateral? Will you find some for me then?" he sneered. In a frenzied roar, Aunt Millie charged toward us. I imagined her missing her mark, knocking me to the floor.

In a sudden swipe, a voice at the back door sliced through me.

"What's going on here?"

Relief did a somersault inside me. My legs felt like rubber. I was never so happy to have Ed Hanover show up. Jim swung around to face him. His hand was still clamped across my mouth.

"Take your hands off my kid, or I'll give you a fist full of collateral," said Ed, more serious than I had ever heard him sound in my life. Aunt Millie let out a gasp. I stood looking at Ed like he was out of his mind.

Chapter Twenty

"Ed Hanover's your pa? Get out of town!"

I made a clicking sound with my tongue to show how pleased I was. The disbelief in Evelyn's voice came through loud and clear. I could understand why. I hardly knew what to think myself. I'd wrestled with the idea all night long, turning over every conversation I'd ever had with Ed, thinking that maybe there'd been some clue that I should have picked up on. But other than the fact that he'd always been nice to me and seemed interested in what I was doing, I couldn't think of anything I'd overlooked. Ed and Aunt Millie had both been pretty sly about the whole thing.

"You know what this means?" said Evelyn, leading the way through the wooded area and toward Hux Wagner's camp.

"No, what?"

"At least you got a regular pa in the bargain. Ed seems okay to me."

I was glad he said that. Ed *was* okay, normal so far as I could tell, despite what Aunt Millie said about his head being messed up from the war.

If anything sounded strange to my ears, it was hearing Evelyn call Ed my pa. He stopped and gave me the once-over, like maybe he was trying to see some family resemblance, sizing me up like a prized bull at the fair. I pushed on him, a small nudge just to make him move. I didn't like being inspected that way, but to tell the truth I'd been wondering the same thing myself. I'd given myself an overhauling, scrutinizing my looks in the mirror that morning, wondering what, if anything, we had in common. The only problem was, I'd never seen Ed's features up close. I wasn't really sure about the shape of his nose or even the colour of his eyes. I was only aware of how totally opposite his hair colour was from mine. I always knew I got my fair hair from my mother. That's one thing Aunt Millie hadn't lied about.

If a whirlwind had caught me up and given me a few good spins around, I wouldn't have been any more bewildered. My mind wouldn't shut off last night. Sleeping had been next to impossible, what with everything happening the way it had earlier in the evening. Not to mention the way Aunt Millie'd carried on when she tossed Jim Merry out of the house, telling him not to bother coming back again. I knew she wouldn't make it stick, no more than she had all those other times she'd kicked people out of the house. Aunt Millie's pretty cagey when there's money involved.

"Great timing, Ed showing up with your glasses when he did," said Evelyn. I had thought about not telling him his pa had pulled the back door off its hinges last night and exactly what had happened, but I didn't want to keep any secrets from him.

"Didn't even get a scratch," I said, proud over the fact that my own father thought enough of me to find my glasses for me. More than what I could say for Aunt Millie. Last night I dreamed up Ed down in the dirt, feeling around the dark for my glasses, feet stepping all around, him batting them out of his way, and it made me feel right proud to think he did that for me.

"Good old Mother made them both promise not to tell," I said. "The thing is, the longer you hold on to a secret, the harder it is to keep. Can you imagine, Ed thought I was better off not knowing? Like I wouldn't be better off knowing who my father was." I shut up kind of quick after saying that. It was a sticky situation to be discussing with Evelyn, considering who his pa was.

Evelyn held a bush out of my way to keep it from swishing back at me. Knowing that my mother was behind the lie didn't change the rest of the lies Aunt Millie had concocted over the years. Besides, what say did my mother even have in the matter, her dumping me out and taking off the way she did? Even Aunt Millie has barely heard from her.

Evelyn slowed down and grabbed my arm. "We're here," he said, spreading apart the alder bushes to get a good look at Hux Wagner's camp. "So you think good old Ed's going to let you go to Halifax?" he asked.

"He will if I ask him," I said with confidence. I couldn't help but smile. Everything was falling into place. A small part of me didn't think I deserved to be this happy. Ed would do anything I wanted. My whole life had changed. I could feel it.

"No matter what you think, Cammie, I always did what I thought was right," Aunt Mille had said last night as we climbed the stairs for bed. She was expecting me to say it was all okay, but I wouldn't give her the satisfaction. There were too many lies pulling down the walls of that house, too many secrets to simply pass them off with a flick of my hand.

Come fall, I'd be giving both Aunt Millie and Tanner the boot. I'd be starting my new life, the one I'd been planning on most all my life. I knew it was going to look a bit different than all those scenarios I'd dreamed up in my head over the years, but I wasn't about to hold out for something better. Even though I wasn't going to be out on some boat on the Atlantic, something told me this was the best it was going to get. It wasn't some dreamed-up fantasy. It was solid and real.

But me getting what I wanted didn't mean I was about to give up on the plan Evelyn and I had already cooked up. We still had to get rid of old Hux's moonshine still, make it so Evelyn's old man would have to stop drinking. Just because my end of things was working out didn't mean I was going to forget about Evelyn's plan to get his old man sober. In a few more minutes, he'd be getting ready to start his next life, just like me. No way was I going to let Evelyn down.

"I don't see old Hux around anywhere," Evelyn whispered like he'd just won the jelly beans down at Mae Cushion's for guessing how many were in the tall glass jar on her counter. "I've got to get going before he comes back."

Evelyn sucked in a big gulp of air and pulled the blasting cap out of his pocket.

"He might be inside," I said. The air tingled with anticipation. The little bird inside me was moving its wings. Maybe this was too risky.

"There's a window, I'll check inside. You okay here by yourself?" he asked.

"What do you take me for, an idiot?"

"Maybe," he said. I ignored the comic sound in his voice. This was no time to be joking. This was serious business in the highest degree.

A breeze came up from nowhere and chilled me. I shivered and fastened the buttons on my sweater.

"Just be careful, Evelyn. Watch what you're doing and get out of there as soon as you light that fuse."

The next few minutes were all his. I had to trust that everything would go off without a hitch. Evelyn took another deep breath and stepped out in the open.

I peeked out through the bushes and watched Evelyn head toward Hux's camp, like a sleek, dark shadow making his way through the clearing. The rest I could only guess at, the rest was something for me to dream up in my head.

Evelyn, grabbing fast to the windowsill, taking a gander inside old Hux's camp. The window is high. He stretches his neck out and looks around. No sign of Hux, so he heads toward the moonshine still. He pushes the blasting cap into the fire pit beneath the still and stretches out the fuse. He feels around until he finds the matchbox in his shirt pocket. He only gets three chances to light the fuse before the matches are gone. Striking one against the box, he cups it with his hands to keep it from being snuffed out by the wind. The match sizzles and he holds it close to the fuse. Like a cat on the prowl he's ready to jump up and start running the second that fuse starts to burn.

I looked out through the alders. Evelyn was heading my way. We were seconds away from hearing the blast. I called out for him to run, run, run. I saw him stumble and he went down. The little bird inside me was beating its wings so hard that it hurt. I wanted to go to him, but what could I do?

"Hurry, Evelyn!" I screamed so loud my lungs burned. He got up off the ground.

How much time did he have?

The explosion was deafening. It came with a force that pushed and strained against the wind. I screamed for Evelyn, so long and so loud my lungs felt raw. Too bad if he laughed at me later and called me a sissy. I couldn't help myself.

Out in the clearing, a strange sound erupted as debris rained down from the sky. I knew the sound came from Evelyn. The next noise sounded like metal hitting the rocks, thumping the ground. Something landed in the bushes beside me and I jumped backward. The little bird inside me was trembling with fright. An overpowering odour drifted in on the breeze—gunpowder, moonshine, the remnants of a day-old fire—and mixed in with my tears.

When the air became quiet, I called out to Evelyn. My words echoed in the aftermath of the explosion. He didn't answer. There was a hollow feeling in the breeze, a hole torn in the air that needed to heal. I stuck my head up through the bushes, wondering where Evelyn was. Desperation filled my heart. There was no room for the little bird to move its wings. I jumped out of my hiding place. I had to find him. In the distance something was lying on the ground. My mind was flying with the wind as I ran full speed toward my best friend, Evelyn Merry.

Epilogue

Paper was doubled in two, creases rubbed into the folds, and Miss Muise passed around some of the crayons she kept in her desk drawer.

"Does anyone need a special crayon?" she asked. Her voice didn't have that usual happy ring to it like any other time when we were working with our creativity.

I chose a beautiful bluish-green one, a colour that my own box of eight didn't have. It was Evelyn's favourite, even though he felt self-conscious whenever it came time to express his creativity. But he told me he thought it was kind of pretty. The colour reminded me of the robin's egg Evelyn had found this spring. It was just an empty shell he'd discovered in the grass and placed over the end of his finger to show me. I'd picked it up gently, put it in my hand, and held it up close to see. It was so fragile, so delicate. I fell in love with it at first sight. I thought it was the best gift I'd ever had. I put it in our secret camp to save. I thought Evelyn might poke fun at me the same way he did when I lined the *Evening in Paris* bottles up on the board inside the camp the first time, but he didn't. I set the shell on top of a cold-cream jar until Evelyn had the idea that it should be inside the jar to keep it safe from harm.

"We'll still know it's there, even if we can't see it," he said. "Knowing is more important than seeing." The little bird inside me had agreed.

I drew a nest hidden in the tall grass with four bluish-green eggs inside. It was Miss Muise's idea to make cards for Evelyn for when he wakes up. I offered to give them to him instead of Miss Muise sending them off in the mail. I wanted to be the one to say, "Look, Evelyn. Look what we made you!"

—

Now they are in a bag sitting on the dash of Ed's truck. Neither Ed nor I have a word to say. He's probably thinking he shouldn't have offered to bring me to the hospital, but I have to go to see Evelyn to tell him the really big news. I know Evelyn is waiting for me to report it to him, to tell him that his plan really worked. I figure he's just waiting to hear that his new life is ready for him, and that all he has to do is open his eyes for the very first time.

If Hux hadn't been downstream from the camp when the still blew up, I'm not sure how I would have got help for Evelyn. But I'm not going to dream up what might have happened anymore. There's no point in that now.

The news about Evelyn spread like wildfire all through Tanner and Sheppard Square. Everyone's got their own side of the story to tell, including old Hux Wagner. I know what people are saying, that Evelyn's never going to be the same. Head injuries like that are hard to heal.

Someone called him a vegetable down at Mae Cushion's store the other day, and I had such a shock when Aunt Millie spoke up and said, "Let's just wait and see. If he's a scrapper like his old man he'll come out of this one way or the other."

Everyone is wondering what possessed Evelyn to blow up Hux Wagner's moonshine still, and if they're looking for me to tell them, my lips are sealed. I want to say that it shouldn't take a genius to figure out why he did it, but no one seems to want to lay any blame on Jim Merry, at least not now, with Evelyn lying in a hospital bed, fighting for his life.

"He'd be with the boy day and night if it wasn't for the farm," Mae Cushion said, "but someone has to be there. Ethel's got herself worn down to a peg, poor thing."

We both got what we wanted, Evelyn, each of us a brand new life.

Me, walking in through the doors on my way to the School for the Blind for the very first time, away from the drunks, away from Aunt Millie and the moonshine. The little bird inside me is chirping happily away. I'm swinging my arms and humming a happy tune. Evelyn, back in Tanner, finally helping his pa break in that sloop ox he's always wanted. His pa smiling and laughing, showing him more patience than Miss Muise ever dreamed of having.

Dreams come true for some of us, but not everyone. I don't need a lot of words to say what has to be said. All I have to do is tell Evelyn what he needs to know, have him open his eyes for just a moment, just for me.

Ed stops at the hospital desk and asks which room. We follow the nurse down the hallway.

"I'll be just outside," says Ed. Good. I have things to say that I don't want anyone else to hear.

"Thanks, Ed," I say, kind of glad that he doesn't expect me to call him Dad. Sometimes I'm still angry about the whole situation, and the lies Aunt Millie told me all my life. I could even be mad at Ed if I thought real hard about it. No one should keep a secret like that, especially if you have to make things up along the way. One way or another, it seems like someone always ends up getting hurt. But things could be a whole lot worse. At least Ed's my friend. It's not like he's completely ignored me. The war kept him away for some of those years. What's my mother's excuse? Aunt Millie might be right, Ed doesn't seem like father material, but then he really hasn't had a chance to find out.

"Hey, Evelyn, how's it going?" I ask, trying to sound as though everything is grand, that he's not lying in a hospital bed with his eyes closed and his head in bandages. I want to speak softly, say nice, sweet things, sing melodies in his ear, but if he can hear me in that darkness he's in he'll laugh and say, "You're talking all sweet and nice just like a girl." And then he'll know why.

I don't want him to know why.

I sit down on the very edge of the bed, so far out that my rear end barely touches. The bag of cards I'm holding makes a crinkly sound as I take them out and read each one to Evelyn. A cocoon of curtains and snow-white sheets surrounds him. I've never seen anyone so still, so quiet.

There are other people in the ward, all lying in bed. I can't tell if they are sleeping or awake. I really don't care. Evelyn's breath is as fragile as a spider's web strung across the morning grass and it scares me.

I thought about the things I have to tell him all the way to the hospital. Some things will make him happy, but some other things he doesn't need to know.

"I'm going to blind school in the fall, Evelyn Merry. And just so you know—I'll be spending my free time writing you. You won't be rid of me that quickly," I tell him, and right afterward I feel sad. Why should I be the lucky one? Why couldn't things have worked out the way Evelyn wanted, too? The little bird in my chest is perfectly still. I think it wants to move but doesn't dare. I take a deep breath and pretend to feel happy for Evelyn's sake because I think he would want me to.

"It's all set. I'm signed up and everything. I know I haven't told you this, but I'm going to find my mother, too, if she's still living in Halifax, that is. Aunt Millie and Ed don't know, so don't you tell. I haven't figured out how I'm going to find her yet, but I'll come up with plan." I don't bother him about the envelope I've been saving since I was small with my mother's address in the corner. Too many details about my life and he won't remember the important things I have to say about his. I take a deep breath. The next is hard to talk about. I'm not even sure if he'll believe me or even care.

"I don't know if you know this, Evelyn, but your pa's been making regular visits to the hospital along with your ma. They take turns getting rides into Kentville."

I lean in close to see his face for the next thing I have to say.

"Our plan worked, Evelyn. Aunt Millie's down to her last few bottles and your pa hasn't been around since it happened. Not a drop. I swear. Cross my heart. Everyone's talking about it. He even combs his hair most days, and cleans up after the barn chores are done."

I can't see a thing, not even a slight movement. So much for this happy moment I've been dreaming up in my head. I want to shake him and rouse him from his sleep. *It's time to wake up, Evelyn Merry. You've slept long enough.*

"He can't hear you," the man in the bed next to Evelyn says. I sit up and wave an invisible sword at this intruder. It pierces his skin and my anger flows into his open flesh. How dare he say that in front of Evelyn, my very best friend in this life? I turn my attention back toward Evelyn.

"I bet when you get out of here you'll get that sloop ox you want, now that your pa isn't drinking." If anything will cheer him up, that will.

Not a flicker. Not a wink.

I look out toward the doorway. I can make out Ed's size and shape waiting for me. I don't want to leave. I was so sure, so positive, that once I told Evelyn everything, he'd open his eyes and smile real big. My throat is lumpy. I swallow hard. The pain is nearly unbearable.

"Are you ready, Cammie?" Ed asks. How long has he been waiting?

I walk slowly toward Ed's brown shirt and khaki pants but turn suddenly back toward Evelyn. Why didn't I think of it before? There's one last thing, maybe the most important of all, something I should have told him months ago, before any of this ever happened. I lean over the bed. My lips touch his forehead, I'm that close. I wait for something magical to happen, for the spell to be broken, as the words come out of my mouth.

"They say birds can't fly with broken wings, Evelyn Merry," I whisper. "But that doesn't mean that *we* can't. I promise you that we will."

Acknowledgements

I'd like to say thank you to my editor, Penelope Jackson, and everyone at Nimbus Publishing; to my mum, who inspired me to write the character of Cammie, and for allowing me a small glimpse into the world of the visually impaired; to my daughter, Melanie, the first one to read an earlier version of the manuscript; to Syr Ruus—your advice and encouragement are cherished as much as your friendship; to Jan Coates for inspiring me to keep writing; to Brian for always being by my side; to all my family and friends for your constant support. This would all be meaningless without you. I also want to say thank you to Beulah for being a believer from the very beginning; to Judi, who is not a writer, but a writer's friend; and to Gail for reminding me that writing, and life, offers us the opportunity to step outside our comfort zone.